DEATH SPELL

DAVID SODERGREN

ISBN: 978-1-0685463-6-5

CONTENT WARNINGS

Full content warnings listed on the last page of the book. Please be aware, these contain major spoilers.

For Ho Meng Hua and Kuei Chih-Hung

PART I

THE RITUAL

1

ON THE TENTH FLOOR OF THE GREYFRIAR MEDIA CENTER, Ron Jarvis lurked in the washroom stall, staring at the food storage bag in his sweaty hand. It was packed with dirt, but he could see the fat, pink bodies of the worms squirming through the muck.

So many damn worms.

His stomach lurched. He laid the bag on the toilet roll dispenser and ran a hand through his hair.

So far, so good.

Smuggling the wriggling horrors past security had been the worst part. Well, maybe not the *worst* — that was yet to come — but his nerve-wracking attempts to maintain his composure had almost caused him to ditch his briefcase in the trashcan outside. How would he explain himself if the guards discovered what he was carrying? Not the worms. For those, some lie about going fishing after work would suffice. But the rest of the contents... what would his boss say if those were revealed? Or his wife? Or, heaven forbid, the cops?

He needn't have worried. Despite the bottomless pit of

dread in his stomach, the guards had waved him through with a smile and a friendly greeting, as they always did, and Ron had ridden the elevator straight to the tenth floor, bypassing his own office on nine.

He enjoyed being up here on the top floor, where those in charge — the ones who wielded the *real* power — lorded over their pathetic underlings like ancient monarchs.

That'll be you soon, he told himself.

But only if he hurried. According to his watch, it was eight-forty-five. That didn't give him long. He opened the stall door and peered into the empty washroom. All was quiet, save for the gurgle of water through pipes and a single dripping faucet, so he ducked back inside and slid the lock into place. Carefully, he untied the bag. The foul stench of the grave assaulted his nostrils.

The grave...

He recalled the previous night's excursion with a grim shudder. The excuses he had made to Marion. The drive to the cemetery — an out-of-town one, naturally — with a pickaxe and shovel in the trunk. Sneaking over the wall, creeping from headstone to headstone until he found—

The washroom door opened, and two men entered, chatting animatedly.

Ron pressed against the thin wall of the stall, holding his breath.

"So, who do you think's in line for the promotion?" one of the men asked. Ron listened to them unzip their flies in unison.

"It's gotta be Barry. He's been ass-kissing his way to the top for years."

"So, not Ron?"

They laughed at that, their piss streams striking the ceramic urinal. Ron clenched his fists and looked at his worms.

"The Ronster? You gotta be fucking kidding me. The boss likes Barry. Sees him as the son he never had, or some bullshit."

"And what about Ron?"

"Ron's the son nobody *ever wanted."*

More laughter. It reverberated throughout the washroom.

"Bastards," muttered Ron. He checked his watch again. Ten-to-nine. He was running out of time.

The men, whose conversation had turned to more trivial matters, washed their hands and left. Ron was alone once more. He eyed the bag, then reached inside and plucked a worm from the dirt. It curled upwards as if trying to bite him, and he raised the monstrosity to his mouth, letting it dangle.

But what if it was all lies? What if the old man was making a mockery of him? The damned charlatan could be sitting in his shack right now, laughing about how he had fooled another ignorant westerner. Ron hesitated. It was possible. And if anyone other than Edgar Charon had introduced him to the man, he would have thought the whole escapade was a sick joke.

But Edgar was not known for his playful sense of humor, and if there was a chance, no matter how slim, that this could work...

"Fuck it," said Ron, and placed the worm on his tongue.

It squirmed, and he closed his mouth, sealing the invertebrate inside. What now? Should he swallow it whole?

No. The texture may be repellant, but it was preferable to the vile creature wriggling inside his belly until his stomach acids broke it down.

He had to chew.

Ron crunched the worm between his teeth, bursting it, the juices coating the inside of his mouth. It tasted like it smelled. Of dirt, and of the grave. He chomped a couple more times and swallowed, then reached into his bag and pulled out another.

One down, he thought. *Only twelve to go.*

~

After, Ron stood beneath the florescent glare of the lights and flushed the bag down the toilet, waiting until the evidence had disappeared. Then he left the stall and headed for the basin, cursing himself for not bringing mouthwash or gum. Or, even better, a bottle of whiskey. He put his lips to the faucet and rinsed the saltiness from his mouth.

"Woah there, Ron. Not feeling a little nervous, are you?"

He recognized the voice immediately. Barry Benchley, his only rival for the promotion.

Shit.

Ron righted himself and looked at Barry in the mirror. Dressed in a freshly laundered — and very expensive — suit, Barry wore the smug grin of a man who hadn't recently eaten thirteen worms. The lingering taste turned Ron's stomach, and he belched. He swore he felt them moving around in his belly.

"Better get something to settle that stomach of yours," grinned Barry, as he ran his hands under the water. "Though if you want to head home sick, it won't matter." His voice dropped to a casual whisper. "Word is, the promotion is all mine."

"Wouldn't miss it for the world," said Ron, offering his own insincere smile. "May the best man win."

"The best man," said Barry. He nodded appreciatively. "I like that. Maybe I'll get it on a mug." He laughed, and slapped Ron on the arm, leaving a wet hand print. "Hey, I'm just kidding. Seriously, good luck, Ron. I know you've been wanting this for a while. And whoever wins, there'll be no hard feelings, right?"

"You bet," lied Ron. "All's fair in love and business."

Barry laughed at that. "All's fair in love and business, huh? I like that one, too. Tell you what, Ron. When I'm in charge, I'm gonna find you a job in marketing, how's that sound?"

"That sounds just swell," Ron replied. God, he hated the man.

"And if that falls through," Barry continued, "I hear there's an opening in the sanitation team."

"Fuck off."

He didn't mean to say it. The words simply tumbled out.

Barry chuckled hollowly. He finished washing his hands and looked at Ron, all pretenses to friendliness dropping from his face.

"Don't push it, man." He reached for Ron's tie and straightened it. "I may seem like a nice guy, but I hold grudges. And I can hold them for a very, very long time." He patted Ron's cheek. "You might wanna remember that." His broad smile returned. "Good luck, Ronster. You're gonna need it."

Ron watched the man leave without a word, his heart pounding in anger. "Don't need luck," he said, as the door swung shut. He stared at his reflection, and his reflection stared back at him. "I got something *better.*"

The meeting started promptly at nine.

Ron and Barry sat opposite each other at the end of the table, separated by Peter Greyfriar himself, the visionary who had turned a one-man operation based in Hicksville, Nebraska into a burgeoning media empire.

"Gentlemen," said Greyfriar — for there were no women present in the boardroom — "I'm going to keep this brief, though I know how much you love when I make a speech." He paused for a ripple of laughter to work its way around the table. "I could do the usual, and talk about profits and strategies, because Lord knows we have plenty of both." The men laughed at that too. "That's right, Jerry knows what I'm talking about. Don't you, Jerry?"

Jerry raised his hands, beaming with pride at being singled out. "You got me, boss!"

Greyfriar chuckled. "And, of course, I could spend all morning bending your ears about performances and deadlines." He looked each man in the eyes as he spoke. "But let's be honest, we're here for one reason today, aren't we? To find out which poor sucker I've chosen as my successor."

More sycophantic laughter. Ron wondered if he would ever tire of hearing it were he on the receiving end.

Greyfriar circled the table as he addressed his top men. "You see, I've been in this game for a long time, and I have glimpsed the future." He paused. "Gentlemen, I don't mind telling you it concerns me. With the emergence of this new fangled internet, some say the writing is on the wall for the likes of newspapers and television. Now I, for one, think that's baloney."

A round of applause broke out.

"I know, I know, you all agree. But you have to, don't you? After all, I'm paying you!"

Yet more laughter. Ron used the opportunity to crack open his briefcase beneath the desk. Chuckling along, he reached in and pulled something free, gripping the object.

Beads of perspiration trickled down the back of his neck into his starched collar.

Greyfriar held his hands up to silence the men. "What I'm saying is, I've worked hard for the last fifty years. My wife would say too hard." He paused for effect. "My mistresses, on the other hand, would say I don't work hard enough."

That got the biggest laugh so far. Ron glanced beneath the table at the rotten, dirty skull in his hand. It was small, a toddler's skull, and as fragile as a crystal champagne flute.

"So," said Greyfriar, "it's finally time for me to retire and enjoy the good life. My successor is going to have to navigate us through some choppy waters, but I'm confident I've picked the right man for the job, and I'm sure you'll show him the same respect you've shown me over the years. Well, to his face, at least."

Ron gripped the skull, careful not to break it. Perhaps the promotion would be his after all? Maybe he wouldn't have to—

Greyfriar turned to Barry and smiled paternally.

"And Barry Benchley, *you* are the man I have chosen."

No one present heard the skull crack in Ron's fist, not over the applause. Nor did they notice him wince as sharp points of shattered bone pierced his palm and drew blood. And only Ron spotted the brief flicker of discomfort that came over Barry's face, as if a passing fly had buzzed into his eye.

Good god. Had it worked?

"Congratulations, Barry," Ron said half-heartedly. "You deserve it."

Barry squinted at him, then pushed his chair back and stood, accepting a firm handshake from Greyfriar. The assembled men fell into silence in anticipation of a gracious acceptance speech. It didn't matter if it was amusing or not; Barry was in charge now, and his subordinates would laugh anyway, loudly and in all the right places.

The new CEO of Greyfriar Media turned to the expectant faces, shivered, and violently hiccuped. His shoulders jerked, and a thin sliver of drool ran from the corner of his mouth.

The men smiled nervously. Only Ron was enjoying the show.

Barry wiped the spittle from his chin. He cleared his throat. Then, he cleared it again.

"Need some water?" asked Ron.

Barry shook his head. He was pale. Pale and sweating. He loosened his tie.

"Well, I've never seen Barry speechless before," said Peter Greyfriar. "What can I say, it's an emotional moment for us all." He glared at his newly chosen successor, his smile pained. "Everything okay there, Barry? The men are waiting."

Barry swayed. He steadied himself with one hand on the table. "I'm sorry," he said. "I don't know what... I... oh God, I think I'm going to—"

Then came the worms.

Barry coughed, choking like a cat with a hairball. The man beside him — good ol' Jerry from accounting — stood to help, but when Barry expelled a mouthful of steaming invertebrates onto the table, Jerry stepped back, tripping over his own chair and falling on his ass. It was the first genuinely funny thing that had happened in the meeting, thought Ron, yet no one was laughing now.

"Sure I can't get you something to drink?" asked Ron. He opened his hand and let the crushed remains of the child's skull sprinkle to the floor.

Barry vomited again, spewing a flood of earthworms across the polished black tabletop. They hit with a splat.

"Jesus H Christ!" shouted Keith Dwyer, Head of Marketing. His cheeks, normally so pink from his alcohol dependency, drained of color as he rose and backed away nervously. Others quickly followed suit.

But Barry wasn't done.

Doubled over, he placed both hands on the table as an unending torrent of the squirming beasts spilled from between his lips. At this point, the men — most of whom had already abandoned their chairs — began scrambling towards the exit in a panic, falling over each other and creating a bottleneck at the door.

"*Fucking worms!*" someone shouted needlessly, as they shoved each other through the narrow doorway.

Ron stole a glance at Peter Greyfriar. Unlike his employees, the grizzled veteran of the business world remained seated, watching the revolting display with a look of mild distaste.

Ron had to force himself to stop grinning.

"Call nine-one-one," he barked at the fleeing men, unwilling to do so himself and risk missing out on the appalling spectacle.

Barry covered his mouth and gasped, "Help!"

Ron studied him closely. The man's skin rippled, the undulations starting on his neck and working up to his cheeks, as if a child had dropped a stone in a fleshy pond.

"Ugh," groaned Barry. One small, brown creature slimed its way out from under his eyelid. With a shaking hand, he pulled it from the socket with a soft slurp. His skin was alive with activity, stretching to breaking point as his face became a mass of writhing horror.

It couldn't hold.

It *didn't* hold.

Barry's face burst open as hundreds — no, *thousands* — of worms gushed onto the table.

He grasped for them with frenzied fingers, shrieking in bewilderment. Flaps of skin dangled from his chin, the creatures emerging from between chunks of exposed muscle, their bodies wet and crimson with blood as they punctured his flesh, bursting from his hands and neck, his expensive suit alive with wriggling terror. They dropped from his nostrils, and sagged from his trouser legs. Barry stumbled backwards, collapsing into a heap, and as his body struck the carpeted floor, it erupted in a hideous morass of bloody worms that oozed forth from the rancid pile of clothes.

What once had been Barry Benchley — husband, father, and CEO of Greyfriar Media for all of ten seconds — was now a tattered, grisly carpet stain.

The room was silent. Still seated at the table, Ron looked around and saw he was alone. His business associates were in the corridor, gagging. Someone had projectile vomited across the frosted glass window, the puke oozing down the glass like blood, while Jerry from accounting had fainted in the doorway.

But where was Greyfriar?

A firm hand clamped down on Ron's shoulder, and he looked up into his boss's eyes.

"Well, Ron," said the old man. "I've seen a lot in my time, but that's a new one, even for me." He took two cigars from his pocket and handed one to Ron, placing the other between his teeth. "Looks like the job's yours, Jarvis."

"Thank you, sir," said Ron. His heart beat madly. "I won't let you down."

"I need a reliable man running this company," said Greyfriar, as he lit his cigar. "Not some pansy who's gonna turn into a pile of worms at the first sign of pressure. You're not gonna do that to me, are you, Ron?"

He looked at the man, gauging his seriousness. "Turn into a pile of worms?"

Greyfriar nodded at him through a thick cloud of cigar smoke.

"No, sir," said Ron.

"Glad to hear it. Meet me in my office at ten-thirty, and we'll go over the paperwork." He looked over at the Barry-shaped mess on the floor. "The damnedest thing," he muttered, then left the room without another word. Greyfriar didn't seem to care what had happened to Barry, and why should he? This wasn't his problem anymore.

It was Ron's.

Grinning, he picked up his briefcase and wandered around the table. The stench in the empty room was unbearable, but Ron couldn't pass up a final opportunity to gloat. He stared in amazement at the worm-riddled skeleton in the ill-fitting suit, and figured he owed Edgar Charon a drink.

The damn spell had worked.

He almost couldn't believe it. Of course, the cost had been high. But who can put a price on power?

"Looks like I was right, Barry," said Ron. "The best man won after all. But like I said..."

He nudged Barry's ribcage with his shoe and watched it gently rock.

"All's fair in love and business, right?"

2

---

25 YEARS LATER

As was so often the case, Nick Pulaski was surrounded by ninjas.

Soundlessly, they circled him, gliding across the dojo mat like deadly phantoms. One held a katana sword, and though the others were open-handed, gleaming throwing stars and sai daggers were tucked neatly into their belts in case of emergency. Nick clenched his fists and looked into their eyes as they passed, waiting for someone to make the first move.

"Hi-yah!" yelled the ninja in front of him, as he lunged forward, bringing his hand down in a fierce chop. Nick effortlessly deflected the blow and caught the man with a right hook. Before the limp body had even hit the floor, the second ninja grunted and came for him.

Nick spun, deftly dodging the katana as it swept over his head. He kicked the ninja in the gut, then grabbed him by his waistband and hurled him against the wall. The man collapsed in a heap, but the fight wasn't over. Nick knew the last ninja was behind him, and he whirled, bringing his arm up to—

Crack!

His elbow made brutal contact with the third ninja's nose. The man's head snapped back, and he immediately dropped.

"Shit!" said Nick. "I'm sorry!" He kneeled by the downed fighter. Already, blood was seeping through the white mask. "You okay, buddy?"

"Cut!"

A medic raced onto the set, closely followed by Tara, the assistant director, her trusty clipboard tucked under her arm.

"Take five, everybody," she shouted.

As the medic snapped her gloves on and opened her pack, Nick helped the ninja gingerly remove his mask, revealing the handsome face of the young stuntman Jason Cheung. Jason wiped the back of his hand over his upper lip, smearing blood across his cheek, and smiled. "Damn, you got me good, bro."

Nick shrugged sheepishly. "Sorry, man. My timing's off today. It's those masks." He turned to the assistant director. "We need thinner masks. I can't hear the stunties."

"Why do you need to *hear* them?"

"We use our voices to help with the fight choreography. Like when Greg shouts *hi-yah,* I know he's about to attack me from behind."

The harried woman looked at him like he was insane. "I'll see what I can do," she sighed, and scribbled a note on her clipboard. "Though the budget is stretched as it is."

Nick raised his eyebrows at Jason as he offered his hand and helped the martial artist to his feet. "You sure you're okay?"

"I'm good," he replied, his Californian surfer-dude voice sounding particularly nasal thanks to the plugs the medic had inserted into both nostrils. "Doesn't feel broken."

Nick remembered all too well how it felt to start out as a stunt performer. The danger, the hard hits from unprofessional actors who failed to pull their punches or learn the choreography, and the general thanklessness of the role. Stunties, as they were affectionately known in the business, were talented performers who were paid to be anonymous. Despite being responsible for the biggest, most impressive stunt sequences, their names were always buried in the end credits. Their job was to sell the illusion, not bask in public glory. And for that reason, Nick — who had begun as a stuntie and now headlined his own successful action franchise — was always quick to thank his stunt team and sing their praises on the publicity circuit.

"You did great, Jason," he said, and hugged the younger man. "Get your nose checked out, and we'll go again."

"Sure thing." An eager smile beamed across his face. "Thank you, Mr. Pulaski."

"Hey, it's Nick, alright?" he shouted back, as the medic accompanied Jason off the set and out of the glare of the spotlights.

"Okay," sighed Tara, consulting the sheets of paper attached to her clipboard. Like most ADs, she wore a perpetual frown of disapproval. "Ready for another take?"

"Not yet." He rotated his neck and shoulders in preparation. "Let's wait for Jason."

"Who?" she asked without looking up.

"Jason. The stuntman whose nose I damn near broke."

Tara looked flustered. She pressed a button on her headset. "No, no... we won't be long. I *know* time is money, Deran." She looked up at Nick. "We have to go now. If we overrun, the unions will have our ass. We can get another stunt person. Hell, we've got *plenty* of them."

"No, we wait." Nick signalled to his PA for a bottle of water, then turned back to Tara. "Everyone deserves their chance at glory."

"Glory? All he's doing is getting elbowed in the face."

"Well, I got my start getting kicked in the balls by Ryan Gosling."

"In a movie?"

"What? Yeah, of *course* in a movie. What do you... look, all I'm saying is, you gotta start somewhere. So let's wait for the kid and give him his chance. Those guys are the next generation of stars, y'know."

"Deran's not interested in the next generation, Nick. He's shouting in my ear that you're costing the production money." She offered him a wry glance. "And you *know* how loud Deran can get."

"I don't give a shit what he thinks," he laughed. He appreciated that Tara had a difficult role — the assistant director basically ran the movie set — but on this matter, he absolutely would not budge. "I'm going to my trailer, and I'll be back in ten minutes to fight Jason again."

"And what do you want me to tell Deran?"

"Tell him if he's that concerned about the money, he can take it out of his salary."

"That's not helpful."

"In that case, tell him to shove it up his ass." He flashed her his broadest smile, the one that had won him the hearts of millions of fans, and said, "I'm sure you'll think of something."

∼

As Nick left the bustle of the set and headed for his trailer, he heard Deran ranting about how many set-ups remained. He chuckled. Deran was a talented director — this was their third collaboration, after *Cannibal Kickboxers* and *Kickboxer Meets Dracula* — but sometimes he needed to unclench a little. Granted, this was Deran's first major Hollywood project, and the pressure was on, but Nick had seen a few days' rushes, and thought the footage looked good. The man had nothing to worry about.

Nick left the set and exited through the metal doors. He crossed the studio lot, heading past the unmanned security booth towards his trailer.

His *trailer*.

God, he really was living the dream. Growing up, Nick had idolized Hong Kong stars like Jackie Chan, Gordon Liu, and Chow Yun-fat, as well as their western counterparts; Sylvester Stallone, Arnold Schwarzenegger, and Jean-Claude Van Damme. Now, after the unexpected box office success of his *Billy Kick* series — popular enough to inspire its own porn parody, *Billy Dick* — he figured he was only a couple more hit movies away from joining the pantheon of action movie greats. Hell, some underpaid screenwriter was already toiling on a script for a crossover between his Billy Kick character and Keanu's John Wick.

Kick vs Wick was the working title, though unless this latest film was a huge success, Nick figured it would end up being re-titled *Wick vs Kick*. That was cool. He was perfectly happy to play second fiddle to one of his action idols.

"You've got it made, Pulaski," he grinned.

And the best part? Carol was back by his side to share in the glory.

High school sweethearts, the couple had drifted apart when Carol went to college out of state, and Nick had devoted himself to his career. A string of girlfriends followed, including a brief but torrid affair with Vivienne Jarvis, the daughter of media tycoon Ron Jarvis, but none had satisfied Nick. And when Carol had unexpectedly re-entered his life the previous year, Nick had remembered why he had loved her so much. The two had quickly rekindled their romance, and within a month, Carol was living with him in his sprawling Beverly Hills mansion.

He paused outside his trailer to reflect on his good fortune. Hell, even his trailer was bigger than the home he had grown up in alongside his mom and three brothers.

"You've got it *made,*" he repeated, and opened the door. He hit the light switch and went straight for the fridge, retrieving a smoothie and—

"Hello, lover."

He sighed at the sound of the all-too-familiar voice.

"Vivienne," he said, and slammed the fridge door. "What the fuck are you doing in my trailer?"

He turned to find her lying in repose on the leather couch in a blue silk kimono, her long hair hanging loosely around her shoulders.

"You don't sound pleased to see me," she pouted.

"That's a goddam understatement. How did you get in here?"

"Money can buy anything, Nick. And I have *plenty* of money."

"Your father does," he said. "Whereas *you* have never worked a day in your life."

She slinked off the couch and stood before him. Her loose kimono hung open, offering a teasing glimpse of her lace underwear. "That may be." She rolled her shoulders and the kimono slid to the floor. "But I have plenty of *other* things men like."

"Jesus Christ," he said, unsure where to look. "You need to leave."

"But don't you want me anymore?"

"I'm taken, Vivienne. You know that. We've been over this before." He shook his head. "Too many fucking times."

She moved closer. He could smell her perfume. "But what does *she* have that I don't?"

"How about class?"

"Fuck class." She ran her hands over her breasts, squeezing them together. "She doesn't have tits like mine. Don't you like my tits anymore, Nick? Don't you want to touch them again, the way you used to?"

"No, I don't."

That part wasn't quite true. Vivienne's beauty was unequaled, and her current state of undress reminded Nick — as if he could ever forget — of how her body curved in *all* the right ways. But he also remembered that Vivienne, spoiled rotten by her billionaire father, was a cruel, selfish brat, prone to temper tantrums and fits of jealous rage. Their brief, tempestuous relationship had ended when Vivienne had stabbed him in the thigh with a pair of scissors during one of their many petty arguments.

She hooked her thumbs into the waistband of her panties and tugged them down an inch. "Does she do the things to you in bed that I used to?" She looked at him with doe eyes. "Does she make you come the way I did?"

There was no good answer to that. Admittedly, Carol didn't. He doubted *anyone* could match Vivienne's unparalleled sexual prowess. Luckily, Nick didn't care about that, because Carol provided more important things; love and comfort and stability and friendship.

"Well?" she cooed, lowering her panties further.

"Our sex life is very healthy," Nick replied diplomatically. "It's also none of your business, so put your clothes on, or so help me god, I will kick you out in your underwear."

"Oooh," she smiled. "You're so *kinky*. But not before giving me a good... hard... spanking."

Nick rubbed at his forehead. He was not in the mood for this shit. "Vivienne, for the last time, you and me are finished, and we have been for over a year. Now, are you gonna get dressed and get the fuck out of my trailer before I call security?"

"Make me," she said, licking her lips, and came to him, grinding her body against his. "If you're such a big, strong man." She kissed his neck, running her hands over his chest.

"Fine," he said, and put his arms around her, finding her ass and lifting her. Vivienne responded by wrapping her legs around his waist and groaning orgasmically. "Oh, Nick! I knew it! I knew you... wait, what are you doing?"

He carried her to the trailer door, and, holding her up by one plump butt cheek, used his free hand to search for the handle.

"Nick? I asked you—"

"And I fucking warned you, didn't I?" he said, as he opened the door and stepped out onto the lot.

"Don't you dare, you bastard. Don't you fucking—"

He released her, and she stumbled backwards. "You bastard," she whispered. "You fucking—"

"Shut up and leave me alone, Vivienne," he said, then stormed back into his trailer, locking the door behind him.

"You motherfucker!" she screamed. He glanced out the tinted window, and found it rather embarrassing to see a grown woman in her underwear stomping her feet and throwing a public tantrum. "I'll fucking kill you! She'll never love you like I did! That gold-digger cunt! That fat fucking slut!"

Nick opened the window and tossed her kimono onto the concrete. "Get dressed," he said coldly, "and fuck off."

Vivienne scurried over and hurriedly wrapped the garment around herself, all while screaming, "You're a bastard, Nick Pulaski! You're the worst lay I ever had! You're a fucking amateur!"

"I don't want to see you again, Vivienne," he called through the glass. "We are over, do you hear me? *Over!*"

He closed the window and slumped onto the couch. There, he picked up the phone and dialed for security, listening to Vivienne's muffled cries until the guards arrived and escorted her from the supposedly closed set. He wondered how much it had cost her to buy her way into his trailer.

"Pretty expensive way to humiliate yourself," he said, and as he lay back and massaged his temples, Nick Pulaski quietly hoped it would be the last he would see of Vivienne Jarvis for a long, long time.

3

THAT EVENING, NICK RETURNED HOME FROM THE SHOOT TO find Carol lounging in their cinema room, Jackie Chan's *Police Story* playing on the 4K projector. Not only was it one of his favorite movies, but the pair had shared their first teenage kiss during a viewing of the VHS back in the nineties. They had made out in Carol's mom's basement, pausing only to watch the climactic shopping mall show-down in slack-jawed awe.

Perhaps inevitably, Nick's lifelong obsession with action films meant the early years of their relationship had instilled in Carol a great love of martial arts cinema. So not only was she gorgeous and sweet and funny, but she liked to unwind by watching people kick the shit out of each other.

Yeah, Carol was a keeper, alright, unlike Vivienne Jarvis, who spent the entirety of their screening of Sammo Hung's *Eastern Condors* making racist remarks about the cast. He wondered if he should tell Carol about Vivienne's visit to the set?

"Hi, honey," she said as he entered the room. "I made popcorn. Want some?"

"God, I love you, you know that?" He settled down next to her and stole an appreciative glance at her tight t-shirt and even tighter gym shorts.

Carol rested the popcorn bucket on his lap and lay against him. They shared a quick kiss, and Nick decided not to mention his psycho ex-girlfriend. It would only spoil the mood.

"Good day at work?" she asked, her eyes never leaving the screen.

"Broke a stuntman's nose, got shouted at by Deran, tripped over a cable and almost twisted my ankle." He stuffed a handful of popcorn in his mouth. "You know, the usual."

Onscreen, Jackie Chan's car had crashed, and he was facing off against a group of hired goons in an electrifying fight scene that had, the first time he saw it, quite literally changed the course of young Nick Pulaski's life.

"Are you sure that's all?" Carol prodded.

"Yup. Why?"

"Oh, no reason." She rummaged for more popcorn. "I thought you might have had a visitor today."

Shit.

Did she know about Vivienne? He had to tread carefully.

"Why would you think that?"

They both winced as Jackie kicked a bad guy into a car windscreen.

"Because Vivienne called me this afternoon," said Carol.

"Oh." That was not good. "And what did she have to say?"

"Well, she started by calling me a cunt," she said matter-of-factly. "Then she called me a slut and a whore, and said she was going to kill me, and that she hated you and wanted you dead."

"Is that all?"

"Yeah." She smiled at him. "Y'know, *the usual.*"

Nick nodded. "Do we need to change the number again?"

"I don't think it'll make any difference." She snuggled in closer. "What did you do to her, Nick? She sounded even more unhinged than usual."

"Nothing much. I found her in my trailer, and I kicked her out."

"Is that all?"

"She was only wearing her bra and panties."

Carol laughed. "Oh my god, that's fucking priceless. How did she get home?"

"Don't know, don't care." He gave Carol a gentle squeeze. "Hey, you want me to talk to the cops again? I don't want her harassing you while I'm out."

"I can handle myself. At first, sure, it upset me a little. But now I just find it funny. She's really pathetic. What the hell did you see in her, anyway?"

Now, that was a dangerous question. Nick had been drawn to Vivienne — like most men — by her...

"Oh, you know. She's got a, uh, great sense of humor."

"Uh-huh."

"And she made a mean toasted sandwich."

"Better than mine?"

Nick grinned. "Not even close."

"The right answer," said Carol. She stretched theatrically, raising her arms and puffing her chest out. "And what about these?" she asked, lifting her t-shirt over her head and tossing it aside. She wasn't wearing a bra. "Are hers better than mine?"

Nick felt himself stiffen.

"That's a dumb question," he whispered, and Carol

clambered on top of him, knocking the popcorn bucket off his lap and spilling the contents onto the floor.

"Hey," said Nick with a sly smile. "The movie's on."

She kissed him, then asked with mock sincerity, "Am I better looking than Jackie Chan?"

"Now, that's a tough one. I'm gonna have to think about that."

"You do that," said Carol, as she pushed Nick down onto the sofa and lay atop him, his hands fumbling her gym shorts over her ass. "You just lie back and have a real... good... *think.*"

4

————

ACROSS TOWN, RON JARVIS STEPPED OUT OF THE PRIVATE elevator into his penthouse suite on the one-hundredth floor of Jarvis Tower. He removed his shoes and fastidiously placed them onto the rack, then left his briefcase on the gold-plated table and walked to the window to admire a view he never tired of. Jarvis Tower was the tallest skyscraper in LA, and from up here, he could survey the entire city.

His kingdom.

The building made his previous headquarters, The Greyfriar Media Center, look like a slum apartment block. A small part of him had been sorry to leave the old site behind, but Ron was not renowned for his sentimentality, and his ever-expanding media empire demanded a head-quarters to match their international dominance. Plus, they had never quite been able to remove the stench of worms from the tenth floor.

He turned his back on the breathtaking vista and wandered to one of his bedrooms, loosening his tie and pondering his vast empire.

All this was his.

He owned more than half the media outlets in the country, and had made serious inroads into China and Europe. The whole world was there for the taking, and all thanks to a bag of worms.

Life could be funny, sometimes.

He strode down the hallway past priceless paintings by artists whose names he didn't care to learn, and rounded the corner without so much as a glance at the diamond-encrusted skull that had cost him seventy-five million. Art bored Ron, but his impressive collection had won him some rare good publicity over the years, so he kept the pieces on display.

En route to his current bedroom — his refusal to spend more than three nights in a row in the same bed meant the rooms were on constant rotation — he heard a faint sniffling from behind one of the doors.

Vivienne.

He paused outside and rapped his knuckles against the mahogany. "Viv? You okay?" She didn't answer, and he tried again. "What's the matter, pumpkin?"

Still nothing, which meant she wanted him to enter. If she hadn't, she would have told him to *fuck the fuck off*.

"I'm coming in," he said, and opened the door to find Vivienne sitting cross-legged on her bed in a baggy Dior hoodie and purple leggings, makeup running down her tear-streaked face. These days, it was a common sight in the penthouse.

"What's wrong?" he asked, though he already had a pretty good idea.

She didn't look up at him. "I don't want to talk about it."

"That's okay, pumpkin. I'll leave you—"

"He *humiliated* me, daddy!" she shrieked. "In front of everyone!"

Ron entered the room and perched next to his daughter on the kingsize bed, running his fingers across the satin sheets. "Him again?"

Vivienne nodded emphatically. "I visited him on the set of his new movie, and he threw me out of his trailer in front of the whole crew... and I was naked! Completely naked! Everybody saw me!"

Ron frowned. "Why were you naked?"

"That's not the point, daddy," she said, and dissolved into tears.

He put his arm around her as she sobbed into his shoulder. Christ, how long had she been like this? That second-rate Seagal clone Nick Pulaski had broken up with her over a year ago, and she was still mooning about him. He supposed that, as the only daughter of one of the wealthiest men in America, Vivienne was used to getting what she wanted, and the fact she couldn't have Nick Pulaski as her boyfriend seemed to be driving her insane.

"Come on, Viv. If he doesn't want you, then—"

"But he *does* want me! Don't you understand? Don't you *listen* to me? It's that *woman* he's with... that fucking ugly cunt. She's brainwashed him, daddy." Vivienne looked at her father with red, bleary eyes, and said with deadly seriousness, "She's *brainwashed* him."

Ron didn't know what to say to that. All he wanted was to see his daughter happy and smiling again, the way she occasionally used to.

He blamed himself.

Vivienne had never been the same since her mother's death, and that was partly due to his own failures as a father. He hadn't been there for her, instead entrusting his daughter into the care of a series of maids and nannies. His solution to her mood swings had been to shower her with money, buying her the prettiest dresses and the most expensive perfumes and throwing the most extravagant balls and parties for her birthdays. But what was he supposed to do? He owned the largest media company in the United States — officially bigger than Comcast as of 2022, thanks to his acquisition of Disney — and he couldn't waste his days teaching a toddler how to tie her shoelaces when there were mergers and workplace harassment lawsuits to deal with.

"I hate her," Vivienne was saying. "I hate that bitch so much. If it wasn't for her, me and Nick would be together forever, I just *know* it."

Ron was out of ideas. He had tried everything except violence when it came to Nick Pulaski. A year ago, the actor had turned down one million dollars to date his daughter again. Six months after that, he declined an offer ten times that amount. Nick was a man of principle and integrity — the worst kind of man — and Ron doubted he could be bought for any price.

And so, with no clue how to make things right, he reverted to his stock response to Vivienne's problems.

"How can I make it better?" he asked, ready and willing to give her whatever she wanted without question. As far as parenting strategies went, it was a costly, but highly successful one.

"There's nothing you can do," said Vivienne. She sniffed, hovering on the verge of tears again. Then, momentarily losing her confident facade, she whispered, *"You can't make him fall in love with me."*

Ron hated to see her like this, especially when the cause of her distress was some stuck-up member of the Hollywood elite. "Maybe a man-to-man talk would straighten things out? After all, if he thinks he can humiliate my daughter in front of an entire film crew—"

"Well, it wasn't actually in front of anyone."

"Okay," he said, "But you were naked, and—"

"I wasn't *totally* naked. I was in my underwear."

"Still—"

"And he gave me my kimono back before anyone saw." She burst into tears again. "Oh, daddy, he's so kindhearted! I love him!"

Ron sighed. He supposed the heart desired what the heart desired, but it was unfortunate that Vivienne's heart had chosen Nick fuckin' Pulaski. Ron knew him well enough. Back when Nick and Vivienne had dated, they had spent some time together, and the man had no discernible vices. He didn't smoke or do drugs, he rarely drank, and he didn't have any broads on the side. Ron was sure of this, because his chief of security Stan Duke had tailed the actor all over town for months and failed to produce any dirt on him. Vivienne was right; he was a good, honest man, and it pissed Ron off.

Vivienne dried her eyes on the sleeve of her thousand-dollar hoodie. "I know what you can do," she said. "If you really want to make me happy."

"Anything, pumpkin." He brushed a strand of hair from her face. "Just name it, and it's yours."

She looked him dead in the eyes. "Kill that woman."

At first, Ron thought she was joking. "What? Who?"

"His girlfriend. Carol what's-her-name. Kill her for me, daddy."

"Are you serious?"

Vivienne fixed him with a bloodshot stare. "I know you can do it. Don't tell me you got to be the richest man in America without burying a few bodies."

"The second richest," he corrected, and Vivienne started crying again.

Fuck.

He could have the woman killed, of course. It was no sweat off his ass. Barry Benchley may have been the first to fall in Ron's relentless quest for power, but he sure as shit hadn't been the last. The messiest, probably, but only because all subsequent hits — and there had been many — were carried out by professional assassins.

So yes, with a snap of his fingers, Nick Pulaski's girlfriend could be erased. But how would that help Vivienne? Did she truly believe her grieving ex would run straight back into her arms? Knowing Nick, he would take a vow of celibacy and open up a charity for abandoned puppies in her name, that fucking do-gooder.

No, for once, murder was not a viable solution. But something Vivienne had said needled at him.

You can't make him fall in love with me.

A seemingly inarguable statement, and yet Ron knew it wasn't quite accurate.

He wiped the fresh tears from his daughter's eyes, his mind racing.

Would it work? Was the old man still around? He wouldn't make any promises. At least, not until he had spoken to Edgar Charon.

And what about the payment for your previous deal? Isn't it almost time for the old man to collect?

It was, but Ron didn't care. He couldn't bear to see Vivienne this upset. And anyway, he had been flat broke the last time he saw the man, and had no cash with which to pay him. Now, he reveled in untold riches. He could strike a new bargain, one that would benefit both parties immensely. Not even the old wizard could turn *that* down.

He slipped his cell from his pocket and opened Edgar Charon's contact info.

"What are you doing, daddy?" asked Vivienne.

"Huh?" He tucked his phone away. "Don't cry anymore, pumpkin. Take a nap. Daddy's gonna make everything alright."

"Are you going to kill that bitch for me?"

"Not quite." He stood, and kissed Vivienne on the head. "Stay here. I've got some calls to make." With that, he left the room and closed the door.

Ron's heart pounded in his chest as he wandered into the living room and stood by the window. He gazed out across his city and called Stan Duke on his private line.

"Duke speaking," said his chief of security.

"Stan, cancel your plans, and get the jet fueled, prepped, and ready for takeoff."

"Right now?"

"Yeah. Viv and I might be taking a trip tonight, and I want you with me."

"Is something up?"

"I'll explain on the way," he said, and hung up. The phone trembled in his hand as he scrolled through his contacts. His lips felt dry, and as he selected Edgar Charon's details and hit the number, he tasted the salty remains of crushed worms on his tongue.

The line rang once, and Edgar answered.

"Ron Jarvis," he said. He sounded the same as ever. *"It's been a while."*

"That it has, Edgar."

"So what do you want from me?"

Edgar had never been big on pleasantries.

"I think you know why I'm calling," said Ron.

"Indeed. But why don't you enlighten me to confirm we're singing from the same hymn sheet?"

A chill ran down Ron's spine. It was a sensation he hadn't experienced in many years, and one that seemed to unlock forgotten, primal memories deep within the dark recesses of his brain.

"I need his help again, Edgar," he said, and closed his eyes. "I need to know if he's still alive."

5

―――――

Four hours later, shortly after receiving a follow-up call from Edgar, Ron boarded his private jet, accompanied by Vivienne and Stan Duke, both of whom were still unaware of the purpose of the trip. He had told them to pack light, for they would be back in approximately three days, and only once they were in the air, and the cabin crew had furnished them with drinks and left them alone, did he explain why they were making a twenty-hour flight to Thailand at such short notice.

"Okay, you two, listen up," he said.

Unable to get comfortable, he leaned back in his easy chair — the entire plane had been decked out like a miniature replica of the Jarvis Tower penthouse — and drank his scotch. He wished his hand would stop shaking.

"I know you're wondering what the fuck is going on, and I won't keep you in suspense any longer. All I ask for is minimal interruptions, and that once we're home, we never speak of this again. Do you understand?"

Vivienne murmured in agreement.

Ron turned to Duke. "Understand?"

The man offered a bemused smile. "You can always count on my discretion."

It was true. Former Navy SEAL Stan Duke had been Ron's right-hand man since before Vivienne's birth. In fact, when Ron had ordered his own wife dead — the bitch knew too much — it was Duke he had trusted to pull the trigger. He was one of the few men Ron called a friend, but if Duke thought he knew all of Ron's dirty secrets, he was wrong.

"Twenty-five years ago," he began, "I killed a man. Now, that won't come as a surprise to you, Duke. And Viv, same probably goes for you. Business is business, and sometimes you have to spill a little red to make a lot of green. I'm not always proud of it, but it's the nature of the game."

Vivienne — who wore Prada walking boots and a five-thousand-dollar safari suit imported from Harrods of London — moved from her supine position on the couch and gazed at her father. "I knew it," she said with a smile, and clutched her Bottega handbag tighter. Ron was proud to hear the admiration in her voice. "Did you do it yourself?"

"Yes... and no," he replied. "Let me finish, pumpkin. You see, this hit took place before I was in the position I am now. It might seem hard to believe, but back then, I was a nobody. I had drive and ambition, and worked my way up the ranks, but this one ass-kisser — Barry Benchley was his name — was always a step ahead. And when the CEO of Greyfriar Media announced he was gonna be stepping down and choosing a successor, there were only two viable choices in the company. Myself... and Barry."

He took a sip of his scotch, his companions listening with rapt attention.

"Obviously, I needed Barry out of the way, permanently. But there was one problem. I had no money, no contacts. Nothing but the shirt on my back."

That part was a lie — he had lived in a perfectly nice apartment, and never went hungry — but Ron couldn't resist upping the drama in his own personal rags-to-riches story.

"At that time, I couldn't even afford a bullet, never mind a gun. But I knew that as long as Barry Benchley was in the picture, that promotion would never be mine. And that's where Edgar Charon came in."

"That's a weird name," said Vivienne.

The story was going to take forever if she kept interrupting, but Ron was pleased she was paying attention. And anyway, how the hell else were they gonna kill twenty hours?

"Edgar wasn't exactly a friend, y'know? I was just glad he wasn't my enemy." He sipped his drink. "He was heavily involved in occult shit. Voodoo, black magic... you name it, Edgar had a vested interest in it. Then one night, when I was drunk and bitching about Barry, Edgar told me he knew a guy in Thailand who might be able to help." Ron took a breath. "A shaman."

"No shit," said Duke.

"What's a shaman?" asked Vivienne.

Ron looked out the window and wondered where they were. All he could see were dark storm clouds, and the occasional glow of lightning crashing deep within.

"A practitioner of black magic. Personally, I never believed in all that hocus pocus shit, but the way Edgar spoke about it could convince the most devout sceptic, and I, being young and desperate, decided to believe him. So that's how we ended up in a jungle hut in Thailand talking to a shaman. To this day, I don't know how Edgar knew about him. But that's the thing with Edgar Charon... he knows things other people don't dare dream of."

Ron smiled thinly, pleased with his dramatic turn of phrase.

"But how did you afford it?" asked Vivienne. "I thought you were broke?"

The plane buffeted as they hit a pocket of turbulence, and Ron's drink spilled over him.

"We made a deal," he snapped, as he dabbed at his pants with a handkerchief. "Look, do you want to know where we're going, or are you just gonna ask inane questions?"

Vivienne's lip trembled.

"I'm sorry," said Ron. "I didn't mean to yell. It's just... I've not been back since that night. Feeling a little on edge."

"So what happened with this shaman?" asked Duke.

"What do you think? As requested, he performed a ritual."

"And you're telling me it worked?" Duke was too professional to smirk at his boss, but his dry tone suggested he didn't believe a word of the story.

"You're damn right it worked!" Ron snarled. "That shaman cast a death spell on Barry, and gave me instructions on what to do next. Once I got back, I had to... well, that part doesn't matter. But it fucking worked, I'll tell you that. The results were... *messy,* to say the least."

Duke scratched at his chin. "So we're going all the way to Thailand to ask some wizard to cast a spell? Come on, Ron, say the word and I'll get one of my crew to kill whoever needs killing. Hell, I'd be happy to do it myself if someone's upset Vivienne."

"But therein lies the issue," said Ron. "I don't need anyone killed."

"I wouldn't mind if *someone* died," said Vivienne.

Ron ignored her. "You see, Duke, my daughter has a slight problem. The man she loves is with someone else."

"She's brainwashed him," interjected Vivienne.

"Uh, yeah," said Ron. "Brainwashed. Anyway, this shaman I met didn't just deal in hexes and curses and death spells. Edgar said he performed love rituals, too."

"A love ritual?" Duke looked dubious. "Are you serious?"

"I know what you're thinking. But believe me, I've seen firsthand what this motherfucker is capable of. And I'm sure you'd agree that if there's a chance we can make Vivienne happy, it's worth pursuing, right?"

"Absolutely," said Duke, because it was the correct thing to say.

"Then that's the matter settled. We're meeting one of Edgar's contacts in Bangkok, and he's gonna take us to meet the shaman. There, we're gonna be on our best behavior, and ask real sweetly if he'll cast a love spell on Nick Pulaski."

Vivienne gripped her father's arm. "Oh daddy, do you really think it'll work?"

"Of course it will." He patted her hand, and turned to the window once more, the terrible deal he had made with the shaman all those years ago lingering in his mind. "I wouldn't be trailing us halfway around the world if I didn't, would I?"

"And what if this shaman says no?" smiled Duke.

"Then we persuade him." Ron finished the dregs of his drink and laid the empty glass down. "And I can be *very* persuasive when I want to be."

6

THANKS TO A STRONG TAILWIND, THEY LANDED IN CHIANG RAI airport early. There, they were met by Sonchai, the local mercenary Edgar had hired as their guide. The man, dressed in blue jeans and a sleeveless denim shirt that displayed his scarred, muscular arms, escorted them to his truck to begin the second leg of the journey. To Ron and Vivienne, who were used to traveling in style in private limousines, the battered, mud-encrusted vehicle came as an unpleasant shock.

After paying off the customs official, they left the airport and drove for hours. Despite the spluttering air con, the heat quickly became unbearable, though nothing seemed to dampen Vivienne's spirit. She gazed out the window, cooing about how adorable the houses and shacks they passed were. After a while, the gas stations and roadside eateries became more sparse, replaced on both sides by impenetrable jungle.

"Do you remember any of this?" Vivienne asked Ron.

"Of course not. It's just a bunch of trees." That was, however, another lie. He truly believed that if they were to get out of the truck right here, right now, he would be able to find his way to the shaman's jungle abode. The strange pull he felt in his gut seemed to urge him onwards towards an unavoidable destiny.

He hoped he was doing the right thing.

But when he glanced at Vivienne, he knew in his heart that he was. She wore an expression he hadn't seen in months; one of hope.

Since learning of the shaman's powers, her whole countenance had altered. Normally, the bumpy ride in the truck would have spoiled her day. But now, she sat with a smile, occasionally nudging her father to show him monkeys swinging through the trees outside.

You're a good father, he told himself. *You've made her happy again.*

The truck took a sharp turn, thundering down an overgrown track at the base of a tall mountain. The rocky terrain battered the wheels and tested the truck's ailing suspension, while the jungle closed in on them from all sides, the spindly limbs of the trees smacking against the windshield.

Ron remembered this road, and shivered as he did so. They were close now, and he began to doubt himself. What if the whole thing had been a fever dream?

No, that was absurd. He could still taste the foul sliminess of the worms in the back of his throat, and pictured Barry expiring in a welter of gore in the boardroom. Magic was not the stuff of fantasy. It was powerful, and it was dangerous, and most importantly, it was real. He knew this, because his entire fortune — his empire — was built on the spilled intestines of a dead man.

All's fair in love and business, he thought.

The truck stopped suddenly, jolting the occupants into

their threadbare seatbelts. Sonchai killed the engine and turned to them, a hand-rolled cigarette between his lips.

"We walk the rest of the way."

~

The jungle throbbed with unfamiliar sounds.

Sonchai led them. In one hand he carried a 9mm handgun with his finger perpetually curled around the trigger, and in the other a machete, with which he hacked at the overhanging vegetation to forge a makeshift pathway. The Jarvises followed close behind him, while Duke — whom Sonchai had furnished with a replica Glock — brought up the rear.

Progress was slow thanks to the oppressive heat, and as they trekked deeper into the undergrowth, Ron noticed a curious thing; all sounds of life seemed to quieten the further they ventured into the jungle, until, after a while, the only audible noises were those made by the small group.

The sun was setting overhead when Sonchai motioned for them to halt. Without the crunch of their footsteps, the silence was overwhelming. At first, Ron heard nothing but the *thump thump* of his own heartbeat, but as he listened, he thought he detected a faint sound.

Singing?

He shared a glance with Vivienne.

Yes, it was definitely someone singing. A woman's voice, crooning a pretty melody in an unfamiliar language. He looked for Duke to check the man was still there, and was relieved to see his security chief gripping the Glock with both hands.

Ron turned back to Sonchai. The mercenary stood before a bank of trees linked by a thick wall of bulbous vines that coiled around the trunks with no obvious start or end point.

The singing was coming from the other side.

Sonchai approached. The man's body tensed, and he placed his feet with utmost care so as not to make a sound. Ron watched him rest a hand on the vines. They pulsated at his touch. Then Sonchai stepped back, raised his machete, and brought it down with tremendous force, burying the blade in one of the vines. A geyser of red liquid erupted from the organism, spraying wildly across Sonchai and splattering the ground near Ron and Vivienne. They retreated to safety behind a tree, as Sonchai continued hacking at the vegetation. Each violent blow unleashed a torrent of crimson sap that drenched the mercenary, and one-by-one the squirming vines fell away, until none remained, and the twisted barrier hung no more.

An icy hand gripped Ron's heart.

There, through the gap, was the ramshackle wooden structure he sometimes recalled during torrid, feverish night terrors.

The shaman's jungle dwelling.

He glanced at the dead vines as they swung from gnarled limbs, the last gasps of red liquid squirting from their bisected ends.

Sonchai placed the machete into a leather sheath on his belt, and turned to the group. "We've arrived," he said, but the words held little comfort for Ron. He looked one more time at the crimson sap dripping from the vines.

God, he could swear they were fucking bleeding.

7

NICK PULASKI LAY ALONE IN BED, LEARNING HIS LINES FOR tomorrow's shoot. Through the wall, he heard the splatter of water on tiles as Carol luxuriated beneath the warm jets of the shower. He wasn't required on set until late afternoon, allowing him and Carol the rare opportunity to spend the morning in each other's company. Nick wasn't sure what he was looking forward to most; the sex, or the chance to have a lie-in.

He always preferred a studio shoot to being on location, as it meant he and Carol weren't apart for too long. His last picture — *Billy Kick II: Kick Harder* — had been filmed in Bulgaria to save the production money, and he had missed his girlfriend like crazy. He sometimes wondered how they had managed without each other for so long after their amicable breakup. What if they had never separated? Would he have still become a movie star, or would he have grown complacent in domestic bliss?

They would never know for sure, but Nick believed everything happened for a reason, and if a few wasted years meant they had found each other at the perfect time in their lives, then so be it.

He had no regrets... other than dating Vivienne.

Their time as a couple hadn't all been bad. At least, not at first. He had, like others before, been swept up in her beauty and confidence and lavish, carefree lifestyle. But as their relationship went on, Nick found it harder to overlook Vivienne's inner ugliness. Her jealousy, her cruelty, her uncaring attitude towards others. He had tried to convince himself she was a good person, but evidence was sparse, and the more time they spent together, the more she let her guard down, revealing a black heart with grotesquely incompatible views on humanity. Nick had been raised with the understanding that all people are equal, and not even the best sex of his life was enough for him to abandon his beliefs.

He broke it off with Vivienne, and though it hadn't gone particularly well — she had set fire to the bed while he was still in it — he had assumed she would quickly move on to the next poor hunk who lumbered into her periphery.

He had assumed incorrectly.

Like the persistent stench of a dead mouse rotting beneath the floorboards, he couldn't get away from her. She turned up on set, and at his house, and called him dozens of times a day. The cops had been no help. Vivienne's father was insanely wealthy, and the LAPD were unwilling to do anything in case he initiated legal action against them. And now Vivienne was calling Carol and harassing her when he was out.

It was too damn much.

The shower shut off, and Carol's bare feet padded along the hallway. She entered the bedroom, and Nick looked up from his script. Carol — like all women, he believed — was at her sexiest when she was just out of the shower, her face slightly flushed, stray droplets of water on her naked body sparkling beneath the lights. So when she walked in wearing sensible pajamas, he chuckled in good-natured disappointment.

Carol climbed into bed without a word and lay with her back to him. Something was bothering her. Nick laid the script on the bedside table and turned onto his side, massaging her shoulder with his left hand. "You're tense," he said, rolling his thumb at her neck and feeling the muscular resistance. "And you're also dry."

"So?"

"*So,* as far as I know, most people come out of the shower wet." He grinned. "I'm told it's something to do with the water."

She didn't respond to that.

Concerned, Nick shuffled closer and slid his hand up her pajama top, resting it on her stomach. "Babe, is everything alright?"

"Everything's fine," she said, too quickly to be true.

"Did Vivienne call again? You can tell—"

"It's not her," Carol said. She rolled over to face him. "I had to check something, that's all."

"Check what?"

A lump. She's found a lump.

Nick's chest constricted. "Are you alright? Do I need to call a doctor?"

"Don't be silly," she said. "I don't need a doctor." Her lips curled into a smile. "Not yet, anyway. Maybe in about nine months' time..."

"What? I don't understand, what are you—"

"God, you're lucky you're so handsome," she said, and

ran her fingers down his broad, muscular chest. "Nick... I'm pregnant."

The shaman's home was exactly as Ron remembered it.

Constructed mainly from bamboo and rope, and raised off the ground by wooden stilts, the hut sat in an idyllic clearing, its thatched roof pointing to the sky. Steps led from a well-cultivated garden, alive with colorful plants and blooming flowers, to an open terrace, upon which exotic birds perched. They cawed and took off to the trees, the jungle teeming with wildlife once more.

Sonchai paused by the stairs and waved them onwards.

They followed, feet squelching in the light marshland, and climbed the steps to the terrace.

Ron smelled cooked meat. His stomach grumbled. He hadn't eaten in hours. None of them had. He raised his fist to knock on the door, but before he could, it opened. His heart momentarily stopped beating.

"*Welcome.*"

It was not the shaman.

Instead, the greeting came from a young woman. Words deserted Ron. As a rich and powerful man, he was no stranger to beautiful women, having spent a good portion of the last twenty-five years in the arms — and beds — of a succession of wannabe actresses and models and adult film stars. But this woman... *this woman...*

"My father said you would be paying us a visit, Mr. Jarvis," she said, and at the sound of his name, Ron shivered. The shaman had a daughter now? The old bastard must have been in his seventies the last time they met. And yet, his genes were strong, for the woman's beauty was almost supernatural. She wore traditional Thai dress, the red and gold fabric exposing the gentle curve of her shoulder, and although Ron was one-hundred percent a tit man, even that small glimpse of bare flesh made his groin tingle in a way it hadn't in years.

Unaware of his rampant desire, the woman continued speaking. "However, I fear you have wasted your precious time. Please, remove your shoes and come inside."

Ron held his hand out for Vivienne to go first, and she reluctantly stepped out of her designer walking boots and entered.

"Wait out here," he said to Duke. He glanced at the man's Glock, and his security chief understood. He passed the firearm to Ron, who tucked it into his waistband and followed his daughter inside.

The stilt house was surprisingly spacious. Diaphanous drapes hung to separate the rooms, and every inch of wall was covered in shelves that groaned under the weight of books and bottles and clay jars. Only an area towards the back of the house was fully hidden by thick blankets. Ron knew that room well.

His brief time in there had changed his life irrevocably.

A fire crackled, and through the smoke that rose to the high point of the thatched roof, he saw the shaman. The man sat on the floor with his legs crossed and his eyes closed, dressed in denim shorts and a Meatloaf t-shirt several sizes too large. His hair and his beard were longer than Ron remembered, but other than that, the old man didn't appear to have aged a day.

"Suwin," said Ron. "You may remember—"

"I remember." The shaman opened his eyes and motioned towards some cushions. "Please, sit. It's been a long time since I was honored by guests in my humble home."

Ron remained standing. "I'm a busy man, so I'll cut straight to the chase. You helped me once—"

"No, no, *sit,*" Suwin urged. He turned to his daughter. "Anong, bring some tea for our guests." The woman bowed and did as asked. "My daughter," said Suwin with obvious pride. "She helps this old man to live out his remaining days in peace."

"Congratulations," said Ron. "You're a lucky man."

"Thank you. I don't know where I'd be without my dear Anong looking after me."

Ron saw his opening and took his chance. "Perhaps you'll understand why I'm here, then. You see, this is *my* daughter, Vivienne." He ushered her closer, and she forced a smile. "She's got a problem, and I thought you might help her, the way you helped me."

Suwin chuckled softly. "Ah, Mr. Jarvis. I regret I am not the man you knew from before. Please, do sit, and I shall explain."

Sighing, Ron perched his ass on a cushion and patted the one next to him. "Come on, Viv. Do as the man says."

Once Vivienne was settled, Anong served them their tea. Ron eyed the steaming container with suspicion, then met Suwin's expectant gaze. He sipped the hot liquid in a gesture of good faith, and laid the cup down. "So, like I was saying, my daughter—"

"Mr. Jarvis," interrupted Suwin. "Do you have any regrets in your life?"

Ron didn't even have to think about the question. "Not one. I own every decision I make."

"Then perhaps it is *you* who is the lucky man. For I have

a great many regrets, but none more so than my use of Yaa Sang. Or, as you know it, black magic."

"Why in the hell would you regret that?" asked an incredulous Ron. "Most men would give anything for that power."

"Oh, I'm aware," said the shaman, and Ron despised the sly grin that crossed his face. "They gave whatever I asked of them, didn't they, Mr. Jarvis?"

Ron felt the gun in his waistband, heavy and dangerous. "I guess they did."

"But do not worry," said Suwin. "Thanks to Anong, I have turned my back on my past life, and in doing so, all payments have been canceled. You hear me, Mr. Jarvis? Our deal is no more. You are free from my debt. I hope this makes you happy."

"So what's he saying?" Vivienne asked her father. "That I came all the way out here for nothing? Daddy, you *promised!*"

"Once again," said Suwin, "I am deeply sorry for your wasted journey." He gazed at Vivienne. "But the man who helped your father is no more. I have my daughter to thank for that. She diverted me from an evil path."

"Well, ain't that swell," grumbled Ron.

"You took the words right out of my mouth, Mr. Jarvis. I may not be able to help you in the manner you desire, but now I am able to live my life in harmony with nature, and you have no more debts to pay me. Two out of three ain't bad, as you Americans might say."

Ron was growing tired of the shaman's hippy-dippy nature crap. "Look, it's not like before, okay? I don't want anyone dead. It's a love spell, that's all."

Something crashed to the floor. All eyes turned to the shaman's daughter. A teacup had slipped from her hand,

and lay in pieces at her feet. "A love spell?" she said. "Love spells are the most dangerous of all."

Ron ogled the young woman. Shit, he wouldn't mind casting a love spell on her. "What do you mean by that? I thought you Buddhists were into love and peace?"

"My daughter means nothing," said Suwin. He glared at Anong. "She forgets herself and speaks out of turn when her elders are talking." He smiled. Did the bastard never stop smiling? "Once again, I apologize. To both of you. But I no longer perform any kind of spell. I have caused much pain and suffering, and I must atone for that. I will spend all the lives I have atoning for it."

"Come on, man," said Ron. "It's just a love spell. You're not hurting anyone."

"We're meant to be together," said Vivienne. "It's written in the stars."

Suwin turned to her. "If that is so, then it will happen naturally."

"But I don't *want* it to happen naturally. I want it *now.*"

"If heaven can wait, then so can you," said Suwin, firmly but not unkindly.

The old fart was pissing Ron off. Not only was he acting like a dick, but Ron was convinced the man kept dropping Meatloaf song titles into the conversation. Luckily, Ron excelled in the art of dealmaking, so he bit back his frustration and decided to appeal to the shaman's obvious paternal instinct.

"Your daughter is a charming young lady," he said casually, casting his gaze towards Anong. The woman pretended not to hear, but he knew she was listening. "You must be very proud of her."

"Anong has shown me a righteous path," said Suwin, "and for that, I am eternally grateful."

"Then let's stop bullshitting each other. From one father to another, wouldn't you do anything to make your daughter happy? To see her smile again?"

"Yes," Suwin said. "I would do anything for love. But a love spell?" He shook his head. "I won't do that."

Ron glared at him, his temper rising. "Right, that's it. You've been Meatloafing me since the moment we arrived, you shriveled little motherfucker." He turned to Vivienne. "On your feet."

"We can't just leave!" she cried. "You *promised* me a love spell."

Ron struggled to rise from the low cushion. "I know what I promised," he growled, then looked at the shaman. He drew in the deepest breath his lungs would allow, and said, "Suwin, I'm going to ask you *one last time*. Will you or will you not help my daughter?"

"I will not," Suwin replied.

"Not for any price, huh?"

"I have no need for earthly possessions." He gazed lovingly at Anong. "Not when I have my daughter."

"Yeah," said Ron, reaching behind his back. "That's what I fucking thought." He pulled the gun free and aimed the barrel at Anong's head. "Which is why I'm sorry it has to come to this."

8

———

"You're pregnant?"

The words were unfamiliar on Nick Pulaski's tongue. He doubted he'd ever said them out loud before, even in one of his movies. In the tradition of Clint Eastwood, Nick usually portrayed the stoic, silent hero, and most of his dialogue consisted of pithy one-liners and rumbling threats. His characters always bedded the women in his films, but they were never—

"Pregnant," he repeated shakily.

Carol nodded. She bit her lower lip. "I'm sorry I kept it from you. I wanted to check one more time before I told you. I needed to be sure."

"And how sure are you?"

Pregnant... she's pregnant...

"Very sure."

They lay in uneasy silence, a million thoughts rattling around Nick's brain like loose change in his pocket. His life, their relationship, his career... everything was about to be turned upside-down.

Forever.

"Nick, say something. Please."

What could he say? Was he ready for the responsibility of fatherhood? Could he handle it? What if—

"Nick!"

Tears formed in Carol's eyes.

He took her hand, and then his own vision blurred. "I'm going to be a dad," he said, the words catching in his throat.

"You are," said Carol. "And I'm going to be a mom."

He looked into her eyes and his heart swelled with such adoration that it frightened him. "I love you," was all he could think to say, as a tempest of emotions thrashed within his mind; joy, confusion, elation, and, yes... *fear.*

The fear was always there.

But the more he considered it, and the longer he looked at Carol, the quicker the other emotions subsumed the fear. For Nick Pulaski was a man who preferred to live in the present. To him, the past was the past, and the future was something he would face when it came. Fear was as inevitable as it was healthy, and there would be time for it over the coming months.

But right now, in the present?

Fear could fuck off.

He pulled Carol close, kissing her and running his hands through her hair.

"Are you happy?" she asked between kisses. "Are you pleased?"

"I've never been so happy," he said... and he meant it.

"Mr. Jarvis," said Suwin, the smile never leaving his lips. "What are you doing?"

"I think I'm making myself pretty damn clear," said Ron.

He buried the tip of the barrel into Anong's hair until he felt the resistance of her skull. "You will cast Vivienne's love spell, or I will blow your foxy little daughter's brains out across this shithole you call a home."

"Don't do it," said Anong, and Ron jabbed the gun hard against her head.

"You have thirty seconds to make up your mind, old man." It was hot in the shack. Even Ron's sweat was sweating. He ran his eyes up and down Anong's youthful body. "You know, your daughter's a real looker. It'd be a shame to let her go to waste. But if my daughter can't be happy, I'll make damn sure yours never gets the chance to."

A moment of contemplation followed, before Suwin nodded. "Very well, Mr. Jarvis. What kind of man would I be if I allowed my only flesh and blood to die? My daughter saved me, so it is my fatherly duty to save her."

Anong glared at her father. "How can you—"

"Silence!" the shaman commanded. "Do not disrespect me, you insolent girl."

"But you've worked so hard to—"

"I said, *silence!*" Suwin looked at Ron. "I apologize for Anong's behavior. Sometimes children forget their place."

"True," said Ron, his grip on the gun never wavering. "But you'd do anything to protect them, right?"

"Anything," said Suwin. "Even condemn myself to Naraka."

"To what?"

For the first time since their arrival, Suwin's expression darkened. "To hell, Mr. Jarvis. I would condemn myself to hell to protect my daughter. I wonder, could you say the same?"

Ron felt Vivienne's eyes on him. He chose to ignore the

question. "So that's settled, then?" he asked instead. "You'll cast the spell?"

"I shall perform the ritual."

Vivienne ran to Ron and threw her arms around him, peppering him with kisses. "Oh daddy, thank you! Thank you, thank you, thank you!"

"No problem, pumpkin," he said, holding Anong's steely gaze as the cold steel of the handgun's barrel pressed tightly against her temple. He allowed himself a small, triumphant smile. "Nothing's too much for daddy's little girl."

"Father, please," said Anong. "After everything you've been through..."

"My decision is made," said Suwin without looking at her.

"Glad to hear it," said Ron. "Then let's get this show on the road. My trigger finger gets real itchy these days."

Suwin's smile returned. "You don't need to threaten me, Mr. Jarvis. I will do what you ask. I will make whoever you wish fall in love with your daughter, and their bond shall be unbreakable." He cast a glance at Vivienne. "Does this satisfy you, young lady?"

"Yeah," she replied. "Mostly. But what about his girlfriend?"

"I don't follow," said Suwin. "Please explain."

"His girlfriend, gramps. I want her out of the picture. Permanently."

"Once the spell is cast," Suwin explained, "the victim — I mean, *recipient* — will only have eyes for you. None other shall interest nor arouse them."

"Yeah, I get that. But this guy *really* loves his girlfriend. We're talking fairy tale, happily ever-after kind of love." Vivienne stepped closer to the shaman. "Make it so he can't stand her. Like, she makes him so *sick* that he can't even bear to be around her. Do that, old man, or I'll take the gun and shoot your daughter's pretty little tits off."

Suwin and Vivienne locked eyes. The shaman seemed on the verge of saying something... and then stopped himself.

"I will do as you ask," he said curtly, and turned away from them. "We begin at once."

9

VIVIENNE JARVIS WAS NOT EASILY RATTLED.

Throughout her life, she had wanted for nothing, and as the daughter of one of the richest men in the country, she said and did as she pleased without fear of repercussion. Her entourage fawned over her, and everyone she met either wanted to be her or to fuck her, which, combined with her unshakable belief in her superiority over others, had earned her the nickname 'The Brat' in the press.

Yet, as the shaman ushered her through the hut and into a shadowy space behind thick, black drapes, she felt an unfamiliar sensation wash over her.

Fear.

She didn't know what to expect. What the fuck even *was* a ritual? She had hoped he might simply say some magic words and sprinkle fairy dust over her, but that seemed less likely by the second. What if the weird old man tried to assault her?

He wouldn't dare.

Her father was in the next room. If the old freak tried something, her daddy would kill him *and* his daughter.

She hadn't realized how much her father cared for her until today. That he was willing to kill for her happiness was a testament to his love. He truly was the best father a girl could wish for.

She took a relaxing breath.

Not only did she have the perfect daddy, but soon she would have the perfect boyfriend. All she had to do was get through this weird ritual, and Nick would be hers to keep and cherish. She considered it a nudge in the right direction rather than a complete personality change. They were obviously going to get together anyway, but neither of them were getting any younger, so she may as well help things along.

They walked into the darkened area. As Vivienne waited, the old man lit eight candles in a circle around her. They offered little respite from the darkness, their flickering light glancing off glass jars containing preserved animals and unidentifiable pieces of meat that floated in semi-transparent fluid.

Seemingly unhindered by the lack of illumination, the wizard gathered items and placed them on a wooden altar. Chalk, bottles of liquid, a skull, and — Vivienne's eyes widened — a live, caged chicken.

What the fuck did he need *that* for?

Using the chalk, he scratched a circle within a circle on the floor and filled the outer ring with symbols. Despite their complicated nature, he scribbled them without thinking.

Vivienne wondered how many times he had performed this ritual over the years.

He finished, the chalk worn down to nothing, and motioned for her to stand in the circle.

Do whatever he tells you, her father had advised. *No*

matter how bizarre it may sound. The old bastard knows what he's doing.

She stepped into the circle, and immediately a pleasant sensation tingled along her limbs from her extremities. "Oh," she gasped, as the strange, thrilling vibrations met between her thighs and remained there. Her body trembled in ecstasy. *"Ohhhhh!"*

She had not expected *this*. Her worries evaporated, the room spinning as vaporous serpents of negative energy drifted away.

The shaman came to her. He smelled of berries.

"Strip," he said.

"Yeah, sure," whispered Vivienne. Lightheaded, she fumbled for the buttons on her safari suit. In the recesses of her mind, she knew this was wrong, but the tingle in her pussy had made its way to her brain, and she felt like she was floating through puffy clouds of marshmallows, mere moments away from the biggest, wildest orgasm of her life.

Whimpering softly, she tugged her pants down over her hips. Not even the sight of the shaman grabbing the chicken from its cage perturbed her as she swayed back and forth in her bra and panties.

"And the rest," the shaman instructed.

"Okay," she said, her voice echoing in her ears. Her numb fingers unclasped the bra and let it fall to the floor.

The shaman nodded, and raised the chicken to his mouth. The desperate foul flapped its wings in a failed escape attempt.

What is he doing, Vivienne wondered dreamily, her whole body alive with erotic energy. She slid her panties off and kicked them out of the circle, her hands dangling by her sides.

The shaman looked her over with disinterest. "Good," he

said, and raised the chicken to his mouth. "We can begin." The feathered beast clucked and thrashed in his rigid grip, reaching a cacophonous fever pitch as the shaman sank his teeth into its belly. He bit through feathers and flesh, blood bubbling to the surface and spilling down his chin.

"Hey, man," Vivienne slurred. "Why?"

The shaman didn't answer. How could he, when the chicken's guts were clamped between his teeth? He tore them free, spitting out stringy intestines and thin, snapped bones, and held the dying beast above his lips, letting the blood gush into his open mouth. He gargled the blood, then turned to Vivienne and spat the vile mouthful over her nude body.

"Woah," she said, no longer sure if she was awake or dreaming.

The shaman took another long drink from the chicken, its legs still kicking, wings still flapping. He spat more blood over Vivienne, drenching her.

"Rub it in," he said, and she did so without thinking, smearing the blood over her belly and breasts. It soaked into her skin, vanishing into her pores, until none remained.

"That feels funny," she moaned in a daze, and when the shaman pressed a finger to her forehead, she collapsed backwards onto her marshmallow cloud and closed her eyes.

She had never — never *ever* — felt so fucking good.

"What's he doing to her?" asked Ron, as the orgasmic moans of his daughter bled through the drapes.

"What you asked of him," replied Anong. She sat on a wicker chair in the corner of the room, stuffing pockets of yellow fabric with a wispy white material and ignoring the gun Ron pointed at her. "He's using magic to elevate her to a state of extreme arousal. At the height of her stimulation, he will insert—"

"Okay, that's enough talk about my daughter's, uh, arousal."

"You asked what he was doing. I'm only telling you."

Ron gritted his teeth. "And I'm telling you to shut up."

Anong shrugged and resumed her work. He watched her thread a thin wooden needle and begin to sew the balls of stuffed fabric together, stretching them into squat limbs.

"What are you doing?" he asked.

"Sewing."

"Yeah, I have eyes. Sewing what?"

"A doll."

"Is that part of the ritual?"

She looked up at him, then tucked her head down and resumed sewing. "Yes. Part of the ritual." From elsewhere, Vivienne's euphoric, blissful whimpers grew louder. Ron wished he could be somewhere, *anywhere* else, but he didn't trust the old wizard *or* his daughter. There was something in Anong's eyes that set him on edge.

"Are they nearly done?"

Vivienne cried out in carnal delirium, and Anong laughed.

"It certainly sounds like it," she said, and went back to her doll.

The shaman chanted words Vivienne didn't understand.

His voice rose and lowered in pitch as he stood over her prone body, a human skull dangling from his hand by three leather cords. The cranium of the skull had been removed, and as he waved it back and forth above her, a green paste dribbled over the sides and down the yellowing bone. Without stopping his mumbled incantations, he laid the skull down and kneeled beside her. Then, he dipped two fingers into the liquid and pressed them to Vivienne's chest.

She raised her head with an effort, watching his fingers deftly skim across her breasts in flowing lines and circles. The energy that flowed through her held her taut in a psychic grip, and with every nimble stroke of the shaman's fingers, searing hot agony flared through her. She tried to make out the symbols, but they were in some foreign language. They covered her breasts and neck, and now the old bastard was scribbling all over her stomach, and moving lower.

Where had the chicken blood gone? Was it inside her?

The shaman reached into the skull and removed a small, round object. He licked the green paste from the ball, revealing what appeared to be a clump of wax, and held it to Vivienne's lips.

"Do you accept?"

"Mhhhm."

"Then it is done." He squeezed her cheeks with his fingers, opening her mouth and forcing the waxy ball inside. It dissolved on her tongue, unleashing the not-entirely unpleasant taste of semen and mangos.

Vivienne closed her eyes and swallowed.

She felt serene. Blissful.

And sensual... so sensual. Even more so than usual. Every nerve ending was attuned to her pleasure. The air on her skin, the hairs on her head, even the wooden floorboards beneath her... it was as if nature itself had become a force of eroticism.

She opened her eyes and gazed up at the wizard looming over her.

No, not the wizard... someone else.

A man; naked, muscular, and *very* aroused.

Her beloved Nick.

He parted her legs and kneeled between them, his prominent erection throbbing with desire. God, she hadn't seen his beautiful dick in so long. Unable to force her numb body to physically respond, Vivienne groaned with satisfaction as he thrust into her, gently at first, and then more forcefully.

Was this real?

Vivienne didn't care.

She was so close.

Oh god, oh god, oh god... she was *so... fucking... close!*

As Nick fucked her on the floor of the stilt-house, Vivienne was aware of the shaman circling them and chanting his indecipherable phrases. His presence didn't bother her, for the louder he chanted, the harder Nick pumped his hips, the flames of his lust and desire engulfing her.

The shaman extinguished four of the candles.

Vivienne was going to come. She wished she could kiss Nick, or grab a handful of that tight, hairless ass of his and dig her nails in. Even the rotten smell of chicken entrails, which the shaman carefully draped around Nick's neck, was not enough to put her off. The stringy intestines brushed her face, dripping blood onto her cheeks and neck.

Behind Nick, something glinted in the remaining candlelight.

A blade, long and sharp and deadly.

The shaman wielded the machete, slicing the weapon through the air in slow circles that left sparkling golden trails.

He raised the weapon high.

Vivienne wanted to scream, to warn Nick of impending disaster, but all she could do was moan in rapturous joy as he thrust between her legs, his hands on her breasts, smearing the arcane symbols across her soft flesh.

The shaman swept the machete through the air. The fiendish blade embedded itself in Nick's head, slicing the top of his ear clean off. Blood squirted from the wound. The shaman yanked the machete free, then swung again, this time cleaving deep into Nick's skull. He twisted the weapon, levering the bone open with a grim crunch.

Vivienne watched in a mixture of horror and exceptional arousal as Nick continued fucking her, oblivious to his dreadful injury. The old wizard peeled back Nick's flesh and inserted his fingers into the wide slit. He cracked the skull, and a torrent of gore flooded down Nick's face and splashed onto Vivienne. Then, reaching inside Nick's cranium, he scooped out a handful of quivering pink brain matter.

Nick's eyes rolled into his head, exposing the bloodshot whites. His jaw dropped, yet his hips continued to piston back and forth like clockwork.

Don't stop, thought Vivienne, even as the shaman held her lover's brain over her face and squeezed, wringing the spongey matter out until colorless cerebral fluid dripped into her panting, open mouth.

Nick slumped forwards, and there, in his eyeballs, Vivienne saw the reflection of Carol's screaming, bloodied face, two powerful hands tightening around her neck.

Yes, thought Vivienne. Her orgasm neared. *Do it. Kill her.*

Then she felt hands around her own neck, gripping harder and harder. Nick pounded against her, his fingers closing ever tighter, his thumbs against her windpipe, crushing it.

Stop! You're killing me!

And as Vivienne came, and Nick opened his mouth in a tormented, silent scream, the last thing she saw before blacking out was one bright, blinking eyeball staring at her from the back of her lover's throat.

10

_____

EIGHT-THOUSAND MILES AWAY, NICK WAS MAKING LOVE TO Carol when the nausea hit.

"Nick," she said, her hair stuck to her forehead with sweat, her lips moist with his saliva. "Are you okay?"

He wasn't sure.

The sex had been in celebration of the pregnancy. Nick, who knew as much about pregnancy as he did agricultural science, had been unsure whether they could still have sex. But Carol had initiated the lovemaking, and he sure as hell wasn't going to refuse the woman carrying his baby.

God, he loved her.

God, oh god, oh god, oh god...

That had been the first sign something was wrong. Vivienne's voice in his head, moaning and crying out.

Oh god, oh god, oh god...

Then the headache hit, a furious migraine the likes of which he'd never before experienced, as if his head was being cracked open like a hard-boiled egg. His stomach churned, and he pushed himself up from Carol's body on tense arms. What the hell was this shit?

Oh god, oh god, oh god, yes! Yes!

Nick screwed up his eyes. Why was Vivienne in his fucking head?

"Nick?"

His muscles tightened, his penis softening inside Carol. Beads of sweat formed on his head, his back, his hands, and a foul taste infested his throat. He tried to withdraw, but each movement made his skin burn.

"Nick?"

"Stop talking," he groaned. "Please."

"What's wrong? You feel ill?" Carol's voice pierced his skull like daggers.

What the hell, what the actual fuck...

He had felt fine until a few seconds ago. Better than fine; he was going to be a dad. It was the final piece of the puzzle. A successful career, the woman he loved, and now a child. It was perfect. A dream. A beautiful, wonderful dream.

So why did he feel like this?

"You're scaring me," said Carol.

Nick clenched his jaw, then his fists. "Would you shut up!" he roared.

Strange... his headache was unaffected by his own voice. It was only hers that sent vicious shock waves shooting through his synapses. Her stupid voice, whining and high-pitched like a fucking cartoon *pig,* needled incessantly at his brain.

Tears appeared in her glazed eyes, wet and insipid and pathetic. Christ, he hated her.

Wait, what?

"Nick...? Did I do something wrong? Are you mad—"

His stomach heaved, and he vomited on her face. He couldn't help it. The floodgates opened, and it was all her fault. Her vile, repellant ugliness made him do it. His red vomit — *all that pasta sauce,* he thought — splattered off her flushed cheeks and dotted the pillow like blood. She screamed, and he retched again, right into her open mouth. Choking, she shoved him aside and slid off the bed, wiping his chunky vomit from her face.

Then she, too, threw up.

At the sound of her undigested dinner splashing against the wooden floor, Nick pressed his fists to his eyes.

What's wrong? What in the hell is wrong with you?

He rocked on the edge of the bed, listening to Carol emptying her stomach. His body was a tight ball of trembling muscle.

"My god," he breathed. "I'm sorry. I don't... I don't know what's..."

"I'll call a doctor," she said. Her wretched voice was like a thousand nails scratching down a thousand chalkboards. Bile rose in his throat, and he swallowed it down. Maybe a doctor was a good idea. He was sick. Really fucking sick. Was he dying?

She touched his shoulder, and he recoiled in horror.

"Get off me!" he roared, and spun to face her.

Sniveling, she backed away.

The stink of her cunt mingled with the vile odor of regurgitated tomato and mascarpone sauce. She looked like a clown with her greasy, stained face, shreds of undigested pasta clinging to her cheeks and forehead.

The sight of her disgusted him.

The brazen curves of her voluptuous naked body were the epitome of foul monstrousness, a sick parody of femininity. Her breasts were the worst part. They rose with each breath, then fell back into place, mocking him. He wanted to cut them. Cut them deep, and remove the evil that flowed through her veins. God, her veins. He saw them pulsating through her weak, putrid limbs.

No! No, no, no! You love her! She's beautiful!

He turned away and punched the wall, leaving a dent in the plasterboard.

"You love her," he said aloud, as if to dispel the intrusive thoughts. "You love her!"

"Nick," she sobbed.

He head-butted the wall. Was he losing his mind? Was he going insane? Her fingertips brushed his skin.

Why?

Why did she have to touch him? Her fingers were tentacles, slimy and obscene, and he whirled, backhanding his pregnant girlfriend across the cheek. His knuckles cracked against bone, and her head rocked back, the force of the blow knocking her onto the bed.

"Don't touch me!" he screamed.

He hated her. Lying there with her legs apart like a Parisian whore, he realized he hated her face, her voice, her body, her smell.

Everything.

She was evil, and her madness was infecting him. It would destroy him, too, if he didn't put an end to it. His head throbbed, and he thought it might explode.

"Get out," he growled. "You're doing this to me."

She sat up, gingerly touching her broken cheek. "Nick... please..."

He threw himself atop her, his hands instinctively finding her neck. They clamped down on her throat. Her skin felt oily and unclean. She pounded her fists against him, but she didn't stand a chance. Nick had trained in taekwondo, kickboxing, wushu, and karate, and although he was a movie star, he had competed in professional martial arts tournaments for years. If he wanted to — and he did — he could squeeze her neck until her head popped clean off.

He closed his eyes, unable to look at her hideous visage, but even the thought that she was there, inches from his face, made him furious. Keeping one hand around her throat, he raised the other and brought it down on her face.

Something broke, and he struck a second time. Her thrashing body calmed as her oxygen supply diminished, and he dared to open one eye and glance at her. Able to still recognize her, he punched her again, knocking her jaw out of alignment.

"Nick," she spluttered, her voice faint, loose teeth rattling in their gums. "Stop."

He stared at her — at his beautiful, beloved girlfriend — and tried to remember how he had loved her before. Somewhere in his addled mind, he dimly recalled stolen kisses between classes and bike rides through meadows, and the way that, years later, they had rekindled their dormant romance and moved in together, so young, and so in love. All those happy memories... why were they slipping away? Each time he settled on one, it disappeared through cracks that opened in his mind.

He released Carol, and gazed at his bruised, blood-caked hands.

"I can't control myself," he said, tears running down his cheeks. "I can't stop." He clambered off her and staggered from the room. The further he got from her, the more his headache receded, and the less his skin burned in agony. He barged into the bathroom and paused before the mirror, gazing at his bloodshot eyes and white, haunted face.

All he could think about was Vivienne Jarvis. About how he wanted her. To kiss her, to fuck her, to marry her. To devote the rest of his waking life to her. And he would do it.

Soon. Only one thing stood in his way. Something that was making him ill.

"That's not true," he said, breaking down in front of the mirror. He punched it, shattering the glass and staring at his reflections. They glared back at him.

"Kill her," the reflections said. *"Destroy her."*

"No, that's Carol." He gagged at her name. "I love her."

"You can never be happy until she's gone. She'll spoil everything. Don't you want to be happy with Vivienne?"

He didn't. And yet... he did. He would give up everything for Vivienne.

His shaking, bleeding hand opened the bathroom cabinet and reached for his straight razor.

"Kill her," his reflections said. Or so he thought. He couldn't tell what was real anymore, because Carol was messing with his brain like she was tuning the stations on a radio. Interference crackled through his jumbled thoughts, and when he stumbled from the bathroom into the hall, the sickness that radiated from her returned with a vengeance.

A savage kick, and the bedroom door flew open. Carol was crouched on the floor, holding her phone to her smashed, torn lips. Blood gushed from her crooked mouth.

The cops. She's calling the cops.

He had to stop her.

Nick rushed across the room and booted the phone from her hand. She screamed, and tried to crawl to safety across the bed.

Too slow.

Yanking her by the hair, he turned Carol onto her back and brandished the razor before her swollen eyes. His headache returned, a crushing sensation resembling two anvils repeatedly slamming against his temples.

"Please," she said. "The baby..."

Of course. The baby. *His* baby. His... and *hers*. It would be a monster. A sideshow freak. He turned his head and expelled his guts once more, stomach acids trickling down his chin.

Then, he cut her.

Nick slashed the razor blade across Carol's forehead. She bucked and kicked in desperation, but he was too strong for her. Far too strong. He sliced her face, over and over, sawing the blade into her nose, her cheeks, her lips. Blood oozed, then spurted from the wounds.

Still, though, he could see her face, see who she was. He had to change that.

Permanently.

He slit her eyeballs open, and scratched the blade over her skin, peeling her like ripe fruit. With every cut, with every drop of blood spilled, the excruciating agony in his head lessened. He slashed her neck, the blood spraying uncontrollably from severed arteries, and as she expired in a welter of spurting blood and slashed, shredded skin, he pounded her face with his fist, bludgeoning her skull until it shattered.

As he worked, he remembered the good times with Vivienne. The touch of her hand, the soft melody of her voice. The times they had spent together, so full of joy. He couldn't understand why he had ended it, nor why he had turned down her advances ever since. She was a goddess, a monument to beauty and happiness and, yes, *love*.

He loved her.

He loved Vivienne.

He loved her so much, he thought his heart might burst.

And when he opened his eyes and gazed at Carol's foul, desecrated remains — which resembled flattened roadkill rather than anything human — he smiled. The pain and the nausea were almost entirely gone now. He was himself again. His true self. All he had to do was rid the house of every last trace of Carol, and then he could call Vivienne and beg for her forgiveness.

The blade hovered over Carol's belly, where the unholy union of man and beast resided. He stabbed the razor into her flesh, sawing her open, and tears filled his eyes at the sight of jellied, amorphous blob resting within her.

Yes, after this was all over, he would finally be happy again.

He was sure of it.

11

VIVIENNE AWOKE FROM HER DEEP SLUMBER WITH RAPTUROUS waves pulsing throughout her body. She crossed her legs tightly until the sensation passed, then opened her tired eyes. Hints of moonlight broke through the wooden walls and cast pale silver bars across the black curtain.

The ritual was over.

She sat up too fast, her head swooning, and looked down at herself. She was stark naked.

"What the fuck?"

Her memory was hazy. She remembered following the shaman behind the curtain, and him scribbling some weird-ass symbols on the floor, but after that, the recollections ended.

So why the hell was she naked? And where were her clothes? She glanced around uneasily, until the bright pink of her panties caught her eye. Her clothes lay neatly folded on a cushion. She snatched them up and held them close.

"Daddy?" she called.

"Right here, pumpkin," he said from the other side of the curtain. *"How do you feel?"*

"Okay, I think," she said, pleased to hear his voice. She dressed and composed herself, then swept the curtain aside. Her father was where she had left him, his gun still pointing at the shaman's daughter, who busied herself with sewing a bunch of shapeless rags together. The old wizard sat with his legs crossed, staring at Vivienne. He wasn't smiling anymore.

"What the fuck did you do to me?" she asked. "Why was I naked?"

"I cast your spell," he replied curtly. "It is done. The ritual is complete." He breathed deeply, and Vivienne thought she saw a glimmer of sadness in his eyes. "Now hell will welcome us all with open arms."

Everything had to go.

Every item tainted by Carol's foul touch needed to be burned.

Wearing rubber dishwashing gloves lest her belongings contaminate him further, Nick emptied her wardrobe and dressers, piling skirts and blouses and dresses and pants into trash bags. He rounded up her shoes, and rummaged through the dirty laundry in search of her things, dumping them in a heap on the back lawn. With each item he removed from his home, the diseased sickness within him lifted.

Back in the bedroom, he stuffed the bed sheets and pillows into another bag, then crammed in any photos he found of the pair of them. He had to avert his eyes when he did that, as her image repelled him.

Her makeup and toiletries were next. Shampoo, conditioner, toothbrush, lipsticks, perfumes; into the bag they went. He could take no chances. Slinging the last bag over his shoulder, he marched outside and dumped it on the pile. Only one thing remained.

Her body.

The idea of touching it filled him with dread, but if he was ever to know tranquility again, it had to go. Entering the bedroom cautiously, and armed with several trash bags, he glanced out of the corner of his eye at her.

God, she was all fucked up.

He kneeled by her remains and readied the first bag. Her head had been pulped, and when he tried to lift it, the juicy mess stuck to the floor. Changing tactic, he retrieved a dustpan from the kitchen and used that to scrape her from the wooden floorboards. Her ribcage had shattered from where he had repeatedly stomped on it, so he was able to fold Carol in half and shove her into a single bag. Then, he scooped up some stray entrails and the slippery fetus and dumped them in alongside her, before tying the trash bag in a tight knot.

With that grim task complete, he hoisted what was left of Carol onto his shoulder. Their closeness made him wince, so he hurried to the backyard and tossed her onto the pyre.

Burn her. Burn the witch.

In the back of Nick's mind, he knew something was amiss. He just couldn't figure out what. The equation seemed simple enough; Carol made him feel bad, so he had to dispose of her. Vivienne made him feel good, so he had to be with her until the end of time.

"Yeah," he said, picturing Vivienne's lovely face. He imagined stroking it, kissing it, kissing her *all over,* their naked bodies entwined. His cock stiffened, stretching out his blood-soaked sweatpants. "Oh, Vivienne..."

He pictured them in bed together. Like old times. What would it be like to feel her warmth again? To be inside her, to... to...

"Oh my god," he moaned. He had to do something about this. His cock was going to burst at the thought of her. Nick unzipped his fly and freed his erection, letting the warm summer air brush against it. The high walls around the lawn offered much-needed privacy from neighbors and the press, so he took the matchbook from his pocket and stripped his ruined clothes off, laying them on the kindling. Biting his lip, he struck a match and held it to the nearest trash bag.

The plastic melted, then caught fire, the flames spreading quickly. The bags withered away, revealing Carol's destroyed body. It blackened as the fire licked her skin.

Soon, all obstacles to his passionate love affair with Vivienne would be up in flames.

He was free.

Free to love again, and to be loved. And so, as his ex-girlfriend's body burned before him atop a crumbling heap of her own possessions, Nick Pulaski stood in his backyard, fully nude, and started to masturbate.

"I love you, Vivienne," he said, and ejaculated onto the fire. His semen sizzled in the flames, and he started to laugh.

Only *now* could he know true happiness.

12

"SO... THAT'S IT, THEN?" VIVIENNE LOOKED FROM THE SHAMAN to her father and back again, the two men lit only by the small fire in the center of the shack. "Like... are we done here?"

The shaman threaded his fingers together. "The spell has been cast."

Ron thought the man looked tired. Older, even, and somehow thinner, the oversized *Bat Out of Hell* t-shirt drooping from his skeletal frame. He wondered if performing magic took a physical toll on the body.

The spiritual toll never occurred to him.

"See?" Ron said to Suwin. "That wasn't so hard, was it?" He lowered the gun without relinquishing his grip, for the way the shaman's daughter had been staring at him made him uneasy. At even the slightest provocation, he would fire without hesitation.

As if sensing he was thinking about her, Anong said, "Now that you've damned my father to an eternity of suffering, it would be wise to leave."

Ron smirked. "I wasn't planning on sticking around in

this snake-pit." He turned to his daughter. "You sure you're okay?"

"I feel fine," she said. "Actually, I feel terrific."

I bet you do, thought Ron. After being forced to listen to his own daughter orgasm multiple times, he was keen to forget about the whole sordid affair and move on with his life. "Then let's go. We have a plane full of champagne waiting for us."

"But how do I know it worked?" she asked. "How do I know he loves me?"

"It worked," snapped Anong. "My father's spells *always* work."

Ron nodded. "I believe you. And anyway, if you're lying to me, I'll come back and kill you both myself." He smiled at the shaman's daughter. "Young lady, it's been a pleasure to spend time in your company. If you ever need a job as a maid, look me up. I can get you a Green Card no problem, and I could always use a lady with your, uh," — he glanced at her breasts — *"talents."*

Anong did not deign to reply, and Ron made to leave.

"Mr. Jarvis."

The shaman. What did he want now?

"A word before you go, if you please."

"I ain't got time for a heart-to-heart. My daughter—"

"But Mr. Jarvis, it concerns our deal."

Ron smirked. That wily bastard... "I thought we didn't have a deal anymore?" he said playfully.

"It seems the terms have changed. Holding my daughter at gunpoint was a poor tactic for negotiation."

"All's fair in love and business," said Ron with a smile.

"Indeed. I distinctly recall you telling me that same thing twenty-five years ago. But now I see you in action, Mr. Jarvis, I sincerely wonder how far you would have risen in the business world, were it not for my assistance."

Ron bristled. Attacking his business acumen? Now it was personal.

"Vivienne," he said. "Wait outside with Duke."

"But—"

"Just do as I say." He waited for her to throw one of her tantrums, but instead she left quietly and closed the door. Ron faced Suwin, his finger on the trigger of the gun. "Alright, holy man. Speak your mind."

"Afraid your daughter will hear us?"

"I'm not afraid of anything."

The shaman adjusted himself, the floorboards creaking beneath him. "You should be. You've taken a terrible risk, Mr. Jarvis. A love spell? For your daughter, who, on the day of her wedding, shall — as per our deal — belong to me?"

"That deal is finished. You told me so yourself."

"Perhaps I changed my mind?"

"Then that's just bad business." Ron shook his head. "You know, you sit here all high and mighty, thinking you're better than everyone, but you wouldn't last a day in my world. Not even five fuckin' minutes."

"How hurtful," grinned Suwin. He laughed, and so did Anong.

Ron did not appreciate being made fun of. "That's right, assholes. Laugh it up. But leave my daughter alone. *You* broke the deal, not me."

"I *will* collect, Mr. Jarvis."

Ron raised the gun. "Not if you're dead."

Suwin looked him right in the eyes, and smiled. "I won't let death stop me."

The gun shook in Ron's hand as a chill slithered down his spine. He wiped sweat from his brow.

Do it. Shoot him.

He wanted to. He wanted to blow the smug bastard away, but something prevented him. Was it the glint in the shaman's eye? Or the unnerving stillness of his daughter?

He tucked the gun back into his waistband. "I'll see you around some time, wizard," he said, eager to have the last word and leave with some semblance of victory. He stalked towards the door and opened it.

"Indeed," said Suwin, as Ron slammed the door. "In hell, we will have nothing *but* time."

13

———

ANONG STOOD BY THE WINDOW, LISTENING TO THE SIBILANT whisper of the grass as the unwelcome visitors began their long trek back to whichever wretched hole they had crawled out of.

"Those men," she said. "They will return."

Her father put a thin cigarette to his lips. "I know."

"Then why are you sitting there? We should leave."

He lit his cigarette with one hand, waving dismissively with the other. "Let them come," he said, exhaling the smoke through his nostrils.

His cavalier attitude riled her. Did he not care? She peered out the window. They were out of sight... or so they wanted her to believe. Her father drew in a deep breath.

"Sit down," he said.

"Sit?" She paced to the next window. "They'll be coming to *kill* us, you old—

"Anong!" His eyes snapped open. "Do not disrespect me in my own home." He took another draw from his cigarette, the tip sparking. "Now do as your father asks and await our guests." A tear rolled down his cheek. "I have ruined enough lives for one day."

Ron blinked perspiration from his eyes. He carried his suit jacket over his arm, but it did little to offset the stifling jungle heat. Vivienne and Duke walked alongside him, and together they followed Sonchai through the trail of crushed grass and chopped tree limbs they had left on their way in.

He stole a glance at his daughter, pleased to see she was smiling, and mentally congratulated himself for doing the right thing.

Now, only one problem remained. His infernal deal. Way back when he had first met Suwin, he had indeed promised his firstborn to the shaman on the day of her wedding. At the time, he harbored no intention of starting a family. He was young and hungry, and planned on spending the rest of his days as a bachelor, enjoying the sweet nectar of any woman he chose. Those with money and power were never in want of sex or companionship.

It came with the territory.

And so he had agreed to Suwin's terms, secure in the knowledge that the day of payment would never arrive. He had been wrong, of course, and though Vivienne's birth had been a joyous event, the diabolical pact had nibbled at his mind over the ensuing two decades. Well, if the old bastard expected him to pay up, he was wrong. Dead wrong. It wouldn't be the first deal Ron had reneged on.

"Are we almost there?" he called to Sonchai, who strode ahead, seemingly unbothered by the heat.

The muscular man turned to him. "Twenty minutes."

Was that all? God, the first leg of the journey had felt like hours. But now, Ron supposed, his sense of trepidation had abated. The ritual had been performed, and Vivienne was happy. Only one task remained; he needed to close his deal with the shaman.

And this time, he would close it for good.

By the time they reached the truck, the group was starving.

Sonchai drove them to a roadside food joint, which turned out to be someone's home with plastic chairs and tables laid out beneath a backyard awning. There, they dined on noodles and pork and consumed copious amounts of beer and bottled water, while Vivienne talked into her phone, making voice notes of ideas for her and Nick's wedding.

God, the spell had better have worked.

"You okay, boss?" asked Duke. He sipped a Singha beer. "You're too quiet."

Ron watched Vivienne as she chatted animatedly with the young Thai girl who had brought them their food. She was showing pictures of her movie star boyfriend, who the girl evidently recognized, judging by the squeals of delight from the pair.

"She's so happy," he said.

Duke smiled at him. "You're a good father. But do you really think it's worked?"

Vivienne let out a bloodcurdling shriek, and Ron sat up straight. His heart pounded in his chest. "Viv? What's—"

"He's calling me, daddy! Look!" She held her phone up for him to see. Ron couldn't read the lettering on the screen, but Vivienne's choice of photo — a candid shot of Nick

Pulaski, fully nude and very erect — left little doubt as to the identity of her caller.

"Charming," he said, slumping back into an uncomfortably small chair that had not been designed with American asses in mind. "So what are you waiting for? Answer it!"

Vivienne took the call and wandered out of earshot, though when Ron heard her flirtatious laughter, he knew the spell had been successful.

"Well, I'll be damned," grinned Duke.

"Lucky for you," said Ron, "I'm not the kinda man to say I told you so."

"The hell you aren't!"

They laughed at that, and Sonchai, who had been talking to the owner of the restaurant, took a seat next to them, sheltering from the sun beneath the battered canopy. "Shall I drive you to your plane now?"

Ron barely heard him. He watched Vivienne throw her head back with laughter, and saw the sly smile on her lips.

"Oh, Nick!" she cackled. *"You're a bad boy!"*

She noticed her father watching her and disappeared around the side of the house for some privacy.

Ron looked down at his empty noodle bowl, and pushed it across the table. "Yeah, take me and Viv back to the plane. I could do with a shower and some champagne. But fellas, there's something I need from you." He fixed his gaze on Sonchai. The man's jeans were sun-bleached and torn, and his sneakers were marred by holes and ragged laces. "How'd you like to earn a little extra cash, Sonchai?"

"Any friend of Edgar Charon is a friend of mine," he replied. "What do you need me to do?"

"Oh, it's simple. We left some loose ends in the jungle. I'd like you and Duke to head back in and take care of them for me."

"Sounds dangerous."

"It might be. And that's why I have a briefcase containing ten-thousand US dollars just *sitting* on the airplane, going to waste."

"You don't pack light," said Sonchai, a smile breaking out across his grizzled features.

"I'm a man who knows what he wants, and is always willing to pay for it."

"And right now, you want us to kill the shaman and his daughter?"

"I never said that. I'm an innocent man, with no part to play in this. What you do in that jungle is entirely up to you."

Sonchai downed his beer. His expression turned serious. "I'd like to call in a friend. The shaman will know we're coming, and it would be good to have backup."

"Call whoever you want. But that ten-thousand isn't gonna get any bigger."

"That's okay," said Sonchai. "This man is addicted to whores. He'll do the job for five-*hundred.*" He held out his hand, and Ron shook it. "Mr. Jarvis, you've got yourself a deal."

"Perfect." Ron smiled. One of the benefits of being rich and powerful was not having to get your hands dirty. And blood, he knew, was a particularly difficult stain to remove.

"You want them both out of the picture?" asked Duke. "Even the girl?"

"Yeah, both," said Ron, casting all pretenses aside. "Kill 'em, and burn the bodies." He finished his beer and signaled to the waitress to bring another for the road. "Leave no fucking trace."

14

LIT ONLY BY THE SOFT GLOW OF A LANTERN, ANONG STOOD BY the window, waiting. Darkness had fallen on the clearing, but unlike her father, she couldn't sleep. How could he slumber so peacefully when they both knew death approached?

If they left now, escape was still possible through the banyan grove. The men would never be able to follow them through that nightmarish labyrinth of twisted, malformed trees, especially at night. Then, she and her father would head for the mountains and make a new home for themselves, one far removed from the distractions of the outside world, and free from the corrupting influence of magic. Her father's use of Yaa Sang had been eating away at him for years, rotting his insides and slowly killing him. Like a drug, the more he depended on it, the more it destroyed him. Weaning him off magic had taken years of commitment from both of them, and now all that hard work had been undone in a single night.

And needlessly so. She would rather have taken the

bullet than see her father doom himself to an eternity of suffering.

Within the lantern, the candle blinked.

They were close.

Perhaps she could reason with them? In her experience, there were two types of men. One was in awe of women, and would do anything they asked, while the other saw beauty and intelligence as fearful things to be conquered. Which type were *these* men?

She had a pretty good idea.

Listening carefully, she peered through the gauzy curtain. The foliage parted to reveal two men... no, three. The white-haired American, the Thai mercenary, and another, younger white man. She was unsurprised to find Ron Jarvis was not among them.

"Father," she whispered. The old man stirred but did not wake. She crossed the room and shook him. "Father, they're here."

He groaned, stretching his limbs and letting the joints crackle. "At this late hour?" He stifled a yawn. "How inconsiderate."

"They're right outside," she said, trying to instill some urgency in him.

"Then prepare some tea. Our guests will be thirsty."

"They've come to *kill* us," she hissed. Why was he being so obstinate? "There's still time for us. If we leave now—"

"And go where, child? You may leave, if you must. But I hardly think I can outrun hell."

She shook her head. "I'm not going anywhere without you."

"So be it." He got to his feet and shuffled towards the door. Anong watched him with fear in her trembling heart. She unhooked the lantern from its chain and held it close.

As her father reached the door, he looked back at her. For the first time, she saw defeat in his eyes. "This is my fate, Anong. The dark path I've walked has led me here, to this night. For you, there's still hope. Forget about magic, and live a normal life. Whatever happens to me, I deserve it. But you must promise me something..." He turned away from her and faced the door. "Do not seek—"

The back of his head exploded.

His long hair shot backwards, followed by a frenzied spurt of dark blood. The gunshot knocked him off his feet, his loose limbs trailing through the air until he hit the ground. Shards of broken skull rattled across the bamboo floor, and when his head lolled to the side, Anong saw the bullet had caught him right in the eye. The smoking, ruptured socket bled messily down his face, dripping through the gaps in the floor before it had a chance to pool.

The American entered first, his gun drawn. He aimed at her father and pulled the trigger three times, firing directly into his chest, the body jerking with each savage metallic punch. Anong watched the American's face, focusing on his expression of cold, clinical detachment. This man had killed before, many times. He did it without thinking; a reflex, muscle memory.

Like Ron Jarvis, this American was all business. But unlike Jarvis, this man's business was death.

The Thai mercenary bundled his way inside. He glanced once at the bullet-riddled corpse of Anong's father, then locked eyes with her.

"There," he said, and raised his pistol.

Anong had one second to react. She blew out the lantern, extinguishing the flame and plunging the hut into darkness. The men fired, their shots lighting up the gloomy space, but she was quick. She ducked and scrambled towards them on all fours, assuming they would expect her to run *from* them. She dodged to avoid the American's legs and ran for the nearest window.

"Where'd she go?"

"You get her?"

Anong flung herself headfirst through the window hatch. She landed awkwardly on the narrow porch, jarring her shoulder, and hurriedly got to her feet. The noise alerted the men.

"Outside! She's gone out the fucking window!"

She leaped over the bamboo rail and veered towards the banyan grove, that maze-like warren where trees grew upon trees, their branches intermingling until it was hard to tell where one ended and another began. Due to the thousands of jutting, gnarled limbs, it was a difficult place to traverse during daylight. At night, and at speed? Almost impossible. But it was Anong's only hope, so she dove in and ran onwards, shielding her face.

The men were close behind.

"In there!" someone shouted. Twigs snapped, and gunfire erupted.

Though the grove was treacherous, Anong forced herself to speed up. The bark scratched and tore at her as she thudded from tree-to-tree, the forest growing denser with each step.

Crack!

She hit a trunk dead-on, and not even her arms could protect her from the jolt. Dazed, she staggered backwards. But she couldn't stop now.

She reached out, groping blindly, and jogged on.

Cobwebs broke across her face. Good. That meant she hadn't turned back on herself. Her head swam from the impact of the tree. She paused, listening for the men, checking—

A gunshot rang out, the sound muffled by the forest as a sharp discomfort stabbed through her side. At first, the pain was fleeting, almost unreal. But when she reached down and felt warm liquid weeping from the sizzling hole in her flesh, she knew she'd been shot. More blood flooded down her leg, pumping from a second wound in her stomach. The bullet must have passed right through her. In the long term, that was probably a good thing. But right now, she was losing too much blood.

Which direction to go? Her bearings were totally lost, and any sound could give away her position in the almighty silence of the banyan grove. Leaning against a trunk, she closed her eyes and concentrated. Footsteps crunched through the undergrowth. She couldn't isolate them. Her only choice was to continue on, and hope she was heading away from her pursuers.

Another gunshot. The bullet hit a nearby tree, the bark splintering and striking her face.

"I think I got her!" someone shouted.

Ignoring her injuries, Anong ran, each stride causing paroxysms of agony to flare through her limbs. She dodged tree after tree, branches whipping across her face, blood pumping from her wounds.

Moonlight blinked between the twisted limbs, and she followed the shimmering, pale beacon until at last, she emerged, victorious, into...

"No," she panted, gazing in horror at the stilt house. *"No..."*

She was in the clearing. In the darkness, and in her panic, she had gotten turned around, and now she was back where she had started.

A body slammed into her, knocking her roughly to the ground.

"Fucking bitch." A man planted his boot on her lower back and pressed down hard. "Glad I found you," he said in an Australian accent. "You almost cost me five-hundred dollars!"

He took his foot off her. The agony was overwhelming, and she rolled onto her back, gazing up at her attacker. The brim of his cowboy hat cloaked his face in shadow, but as he turned his head, she caught a fleeting glimpse of reflected moonlight in his leering eyes. Furtively, he glanced left and right.

She knew why. When a man checks his surroundings like that, women instinctively know what he's thinking.

Can I get away with it?

He pointed his handgun at her, but he wouldn't shoot her until the others arrived. Men like him demanded an audience for their violence, and for now, he had a different, more intimate cruelty in mind.

He unbuckled his pants and let them sag below his balls. She could smell them.

"Is it true what they say about you?" he asked, as he crouched before her. Grabbing two handfuls of her dress, he tore it open to her waist. "That you're a witch?"

She tried to speak, but all that came out was an incoherent mumble.

The man leaned closer. She felt his penis brush her thigh. "Did you say something?"

Anong glared at him, and forced the words out. *"I'm going to kill you,"* she wheezed, tasting blood in her mouth. *"You... and everyone... you've ever loved."*

15

STAN DUKE WAS IN A ROTTEN MOOD WHEN HE FOUGHT HIS WAY
out of the trees and into the clearing. Blood and sweat stung
his eyes, and shallow scratches criss-crossed his arms. What
a miserable, inhospitable place this was! All he wanted was
to kill the girl, burn the bodies, and return to LA, where it
was possible to assassinate someone without having to
crawl through spider-infested hell-holes.

Light flickered in the hut, and Duke allowed himself a
smile as he stalked towards it. The mission was almost
complete. From within the jungle, he had heard the men
capture the shaman's daughter, and followed the commo-
tion until he reached the clearing. Hopefully, she would be
dead by the time he got there. If not, he would finish her off
himself.

He climbed the stairs on aching legs. Christ, he was
getting too old for this. Next year, he would turn sixty. How
much longer could he keep it up? It wasn't as if he *enjoyed*
killing. To him, it was simply a profession he had been born
with the skills to excel at. He never questioned his superiors'
orders, and could kill anyone — men, women, children,

even animals — without blinking an eyelid. He had no conscience, but Duke did not view that as a bad thing. Like his boss, he considered morality and empathy traits of the feeble-minded.

This was why, when he stepped over the bullet-ridden corpse of the girl's father and saw the unconscious young woman lying naked and beaten, and the mercenaries kneeling on either side of her, he calmly took a seat and lit a cigarette.

"What the fuck are you doing?" he asked, squinting through the smoke at the men.

Sonchai crouched next to the woman, pressing two fingers deep into a bleeding hole in her stomach. The other man — an Australian by the name of Woods, who Sonchai had insisted was trustworthy — watched with his dick in his hands and a shit-eating grin on his face. Sonchai twisted his fingers inside the shaman's daughter as if turning a key.

"You trying to get the bullet out?" asked Duke. He couldn't believe the effort the man was going to for his trophy. With ten-thousand bucks, he could buy as much ammunition as he wanted.

Sonchai didn't look up. Instead, with a soggy squelch, he pressed his fingers in further. The woman groaned.

"He's widening the hole," Woods explained.

"I can see that," said Duke. "Just kill her, and we can leave. There's no need to waste our fucking time torturing her."

Sonchai's lips curled into a grim smile. He inserted his fingers up to the knuckles. "It's not torture." He turned to Duke. "You ever fuck a sorceress?"

Duke flicked the ash from his cigarette, and said nothing.

"Of course you haven't." Sonchai shook his head.

"Fucking a sorceress is like cooking a rare delicacy. You have to do it right."

"Is that what you call fucking?" Duke watched the man slide his fingers in and out of her stomach. "I know an easier way to do it."

Sonchai laughed. "No, you misunderstand, my friend. You cannot fuck a sorceress in the *usual* place, as my colleague here was about to do before I stopped him." His expression grew serious. "The womanly hole is where she stores her powers." He slipped his wet fingers free from her wound. Blood dripped from the tips, leaving an uneven pattern across the woman's thighs. He leaned over and inspected her flesh. "You have to make your *own* hole. She already had one from the bullet, but I wasn't going to fit."

Duke nodded. "Right. But why do you keep calling her a sorceress? She's just the old man's daughter."

"Ah, but the daughter of a powerful shaman will also carry the burden of magic. She may not know how to use her powers, but you cannot be too careful." Sonchai unbuttoned his fly and tugged his jeans and shorts down, smearing her blood over his semi-erect cock. "I'll go first. You two can use the same hole, or make another."

"I'll use the same," said Woods. "Don't matter to me."

"I'll sit this one out," said Duke. "Just get it over with."

Out of morbid curiosity, he watched as Sonchai maneuvred into position, angling his erection towards the bullet wound. He shoved it in, the displaced blood trickling over the woman's bare skin with the revolting sound of a wet mop squeezing against the floor. She was still alive, but barely. Duke wondered if she was even aware of Sonchai's actions.

Skin slapped against skin, and Duke checked his watch. Almost midnight. Ignoring the rhythmic thrusts of the mercenary's hairy ass, he wandered throughout the shack, tearing down the drapes and gathering every piece of clothing and fabric he found. He bundled them together in the middle of the floor.

"Buddy, you've got thirty seconds before I burn this place to the ground."

"The fuck you will," said Woods. "I'm up next."

Duke glanced at the woman. She was deathly pale. "Looks like you're too late."

"No," Sonchai grunted. "Her sexual powers will remain long after her body dies." He didn't seem to care he was screwing a corpse, and Duke was unsurprised. He had known a great many mercenaries in his time, and most of them were seriously fucked in the head. Necrophilia was nothing compared to what some of those guys got up to behind closed doors.

Sonchai's ass flexed, his limbs stiffening. He uttered a guttural cry.

"Are we done?" asked Duke.

Sonchai withdrew with a wet slurp, and rolled to face Duke, his genitals and pubic hair drenched in blood. He licked his lips. "Done," he said. "Sure you don't want to—"

"The fuck I do," said Duke. "Call me old-fashioned, but I like my pussy warm."

"How about you?" Sonchai asked Woods.

"*Shit,*" the man muttered. White fluid glistened on his shirt and dribbled from the tip of his dick. "Can we wait another half hour?"

Duke flicked the wheel of the lighter. "No we absolutely fucking *cannot.*"

He held the naked flame to the pile of fabric. The flammable material sparked, then caught fire. The blaze grew quickly, forcing Duke to step back. He stole a glance at the shaman — the bastard's feet were already on fire — then peered through the orange flames at the woman. Yeah, she was dead, alright.

"Let's go," said Duke.

Sonchai and Woods hauled their pants up and followed him outside. There, the three killers watched as the thatched roof went up in flames. Light gray smoke plumed from the blaze, and as the heat drove them back, Duke could swear that the flames burned white, then purple, and then, lastly, a dark, bloody red.

"I've seen enough," he said, and turned to Sonchai. The crotch of the man's jeans was dark with blood. "I've got a plane to catch."

Inside the burning shack, Anong opened her eyes.

The men were gone.

Those bastards.

Those sick, evil bastards. She inhaled a rasping breath and tried to sit. All around her burned. Her childhood home. Her memories. Her beloved father. She smelled him as the flames wantonly consumed him, cooking his skin to a black and crispy char.

There was no way out. The fire would claim her next.

She had to act fast.

Her fingers found the wide bullet hole where the mercenary had desecrated her with his loathsome member. She pinched the skin around the hole and cried out in pain. It was okay. Even if the men were still out there, they wouldn't hear her over the blaze. Pinching harder, she held her palm above the wound and murmured phrases that meant nothing to the uninitiated.

She hadn't learned the phrases from books, or from her father.

She hadn't needed to.

For once in every generation, a child was born into the world with an intuitive understanding of the ancient knowledge. It had to be this way, for none who studied the old magic could resist the madness and horror that total comprehension brought. Anong had never told her father, but she suspected he knew, and feared her. Why else would he have heeded her pleas to give up magic and live a life of repentance?

She pulled her hand away from her wound. Her insides squirmed. Blood spurted and sizzled in the advancing flames. Then, out it came.

The man's semen.

His ejaculate frothed to the surface, expelled by sheer force of will. She scooped the sticky mass up with her fingers and, leaving a trail of blood that would herald the death of a lesser being, crawled to the corner of the room, where the fabric doll she had constructed during the ritual lay face-down on the floor.

Anong hugged the doll to her bosom. Even as she smeared the man's seed over the fabric and watched it harden like wax, the doll looked so innocent, like a child's toy. And in most people's hands, that's exactly what it would be.

But not hers.

She took a last, loving look at her father — his hair was gone, his skin melting from his face — and gripped the totem.

"This is for you," she said, and despite her father's death, and her hideous violation at the hands of those men, she smiled. They had tried to silence her. They had tried to kill her. But in the end, they had succeeded only in forcibly freeing her from the shackles she had chosen to bind her.

For the sorceress Anong — fully aware of the dangerous, obscene powers that burned within her — had long-ago settled on a path of virtuousness. She had believed that good people could make a difference in the world by showing kindness and nobility, and that love was the most powerful magic of all.

She understood now that she had been wrong.

Kindness hadn't stopped the American from shooting her father point blank in the face.

Nobility hadn't helped her as they raped her dying body.

And as for love?

Well, what use was love against those who had none in their hearts?

She gripped the doll tightly.

Her whole life had been spent trying to change her father, to set him on the right path. And she had failed.

She would not make that mistake again.

These men — these murderers, these rapists — could not be changed. In their attempt to destroy her, they had inadvertently given Anong a new purpose, a new reason to live.

Revenge.

She would hurt them. She would ruin their lives. And then, when she was ready, she would kill them all.

Not for what they had done to her.

Not for what they had done to her father.

And not for all the others they had wronged.

She would do it... because she *could*.

16

DUKE STOMPED THROUGH THE UNDERGROWTH, TRAILING behind Sonchai and Woods as the two men joked about their conquest. All that remained now was for Sonchai to drive them back to the plane, where Ron and Vivienne waited. Ron would pay the mercenaries, and then they were free to leave this godforsaken place for good.

It couldn't come soon enough.

The private jet came fitted with a shower, and Duke wanted nothing more than to scrub the sweat and grime from his body. He supposed he was getting soft in his old age. A spot of dirt never used to bother him back in his military days, but spending time with Ron had gotten him accustomed to a different lifestyle. Expensive suits, fine dining, and finer women were preferable to rolling around in mud or sand with a bunch of men, and the price was as easy as ensuring his boss's safety and occasionally plugging some poor sucker to shut him up.

At least this hit had proven to be more interesting than most. It wasn't every day he got to kill a shaman. Did he believe in the man's powers? Maybe. Duke had seen too much weird shit over the years to dismiss such claims out of hand, but he was unconcerned with any threat of reprisal. The man and his daughter were dead, and though he couldn't condone the actions of Sonchai — Duke preferred to kill quickly and not linger — he had to admit the man had never wavered in his willingness to get the job done, and that earned him Duke's grudging respect. As for Woods? The Australian had no business being here. Duke considered killing him, and decided against it. Though one witness was better than two witnesses, he was exhausted, and that hot shower was calling to him.

They arrived at Sonchai's truck. Duke leaned against the scorching metal, wiping his brow with a forearm dotted with dozens of angry mosquito bites. He scratched at them, relishing the all-too-brief relief it offered.

"One minute," said Sonchai. He stood by a tree and undid his fly.

Duke closed his eyes as the man started pissing. Couldn't he have let them into the vehicle first? Then at least they could have switched on the air con. The damn thing was probably a sweatbox.

"Christ, I'll be glad to get out of here," said Woods. "Anyone got a smoke?"

"No," said Duke.

Woods shrugged, and pulled out his own packet of cigarettes. "That chick was really something, eh?" He lit up. "Wouldn't have minded a ride on that."

Duke said nothing. The more the man spoke, the closer he edged to death.

"Wish we coulda stayed a bit longer," Woods continued. He took a long draw on his smoke. "Never rooted a witch before. We don't have 'em back home, y'see. We got bitches, but no witches." He laughed heartily at that, but when he received no response from Duke, he said, "You got a stick up your arse, mate?"

"I just want to leave. My boss is waiting for me, and he's not a patient man."

"Oh yeah? Bootlicker, eh?"

Duke turned to him. "Say that again, motherfucker."

"Just kiddin' on, mate! Bit of fun, after you cockblocked me—"

"*Ow!*"

The cry came from Sonchai. Both men looked at him, their simmering feud momentarily set aside.

"You done?" asked Duke. "Then quit playing with it so I can go home."

But the mercenary remained by the tree. His shoulder jerked, and he turned his head to look at it, drawing in a sharp breath.

Duke watched him closely. His hand hovered over the gun in his pocket. Something was wrong. "What's the fucking holdup?"

"You constipated?" asked Woods. "You reckon it's the witch's curse?"

Sonchai glared at his shoulder like he'd never noticed it before. The bone spasmed again, and this time the mercenary let out a piercing yell that froze the blood in Duke's veins. It was the sort of high-pitched scream he'd expect to hear from a child, not a jungle-dwelling sociopath. Sonchai's arm suddenly went horizontal, as if someone was...

"*Fuck!!*" the man shouted, and his shoulder cracked. It sounded like a bag of chips being crushed under a tire. Reflexively, Duke drew the Glock. "Hey, Sonchai—"

"*Yeeee-aargh!*"

The mercenary's arm stretched out as if reaching for

something, his fingers grasping at thin air. The limb twisted around, going a full three-sixty, the bones popping and grinding together. Sonchai dropped to his knees, shrieking profanities. Blood soaked his shirt, and then, just as Duke thought the grisly spectacle could get no worse, came the macabre sound of flesh splitting and ripping apart. Sonchai's arm kept turning. Duke considered putting a bullet between the man's eyes and ending his torment, but a certain ghoulish fascination prevented him.

"What's the bastard doing?" asked Woods.

But Duke knew it was the wrong question to ask. Sonchai wasn't *doing* anything... someone else was doing it *to* him.

His arm popped from its socket. The loose limb thudded to the ground, broken bone jutting from the tattered stump.

It came again; the sound of muscles tearing, and of the rending of skin. Sonchai kneeled before Duke and Woods, his other arm rotating. Blood poured from his mouth, and Duke saw the deep grooves of teeth marks in the man's tongue. His eyes begged for help, and, out of respect for the mercenary, Duke aimed the Glock and fired.

The bullet caught the man on the bridge of his nose. His face burst open and he slumped backwards, the shot killing him instantly.

Apparently, no one had told his limbs.

His arm continued to rotate, and one leg stretched, turning back and forth.

"Jesus Christ," said Woods. The Aussie tried to open the truck door. The handle wouldn't budge. "It's locked," he said, and turned to Duke. "And bloody Son's got the keys."

"Course he fucking does," grumbled Duke.

Woods made no move, so Duke stealthily approached the surprisingly active corpse. Sonchai's second arm had snapped off, and lay twitching on the grass. His leg spun at the knee, the bones crackling and snapping like twigs burning in a campfire. Avoiding the slowly turning leg, Duke patted the pockets of Sonchai's blood-drenched jeans. He found the keys, took them, and backed away.

Before he unlocked the truck, he wiped his prints from the Glock and hurled the weapon into the jungle. Woods had moved closer to Sonchai, and stood, staring at the man.

"Oh god," he kept repeating, and when Duke took a last look at the mutilated body, he saw Sonchai's head was twisting all the way around of its own accord. Woods vomited.

"Fucking amateur," Duke muttered, and got in the truck. At the roar of the engine, Woods looked up from his crouched position and stared at him through the windshield.

"Hey!" the man shouted, but Duke was through with the whole damn thing. He put the truck in reverse — it had been a long time since he had used a manual stick — and slammed the pedal. The Australian gave chase, but soon conceded when he had to throw up again.

After a few minutes of reversing along the narrow jungle track, Duke found a space wide enough to turn, and then he was off. In a few hours, he would be back on the plane, enjoying a shower and some hard liquor, perhaps even at the same time. Then, when he got home, he would hire one of his favorite whores and lose himself between her legs for the evening.

Anything to distract him from Sonchai's unnatural demise.

He punched his destination into his iPhone and turned on the truck radio, adjusting the dial until he found an easy listening station. Despite the smooth jazz, sinister thoughts plagued his mind for the duration of the drive. What if the shaman was still alive? He should have examined the corpses more thoroughly. Hell, he shouldn't have left until both bodies were reduced to ash. There were a lot of things he should have done, but he had been so hellbent on getting home and returning to his comfortable, luxurious life that he had neglected his most basic duties.

There's still time to go back, he thought.

No way. Everything was fine. *He* was fine. Sonchai may be lying in several broken pieces, but Duke felt good. In control. If someone wanted to kill him using magic, they had their chance. Going back would only place him in the firing line. It was better to put as much distance between himself and the jungle as possible. Ron would be waiting for him, and he couldn't let his boss down.

As he drove, he grappled with whether to tell Ron what had happened, eventually deciding against it. He would explain that Sonchai and Woods had attempted a double-cross, and that he had defended himself. Ron wouldn't care. It would save him ten-thousand dollars.

And as Duke navigated the rural backroads of Thailand, stopping only once to pick up a cool beer, he glanced in his rearview at the pillar of smoke rising from deep within the trees.

"We *definitely* killed him," he said, in an attempt to convince himself it was over. It had to be. He had shot the old wizard once in the face, three times in the chest, and then set him on fire.

Magic or no magic, no fucker could have survived *that*.

17

Onboard his jet, Ron Jarvis — in a brand new silk shirt and comfortable slacks — reclined on the couch with a fat cigar and a glass of scotch. His freshly showered daughter sat opposite him, wrapped in a towel with a love-struck grin on her face. Like rain drumming on a windowpane, her fingernails rhythmically tapped against her phone screen.

Duke was elsewhere, and Ron was glad to be rid of the man for a while. This was supposed to be a happy occasion, yet his security chief's hangdog expression and haunted eyes were spoiling the mood. Sure, he had killed a few people, but so what? Duke was no stranger to murder. It was what Ron paid him for.

He stole a glance at Vivienne. With her delicate bone structure, full lips, and long legs, she resembled her mother. He watched her for a while, as she smiled and giggled and stared at her phone, and felt like a proper father. A *fine* father.

I did that, he thought. *I made her happy.*

But more importantly, Suwin's death also meant the termination of their contract. His daughter's soul was safe.

The deal was void.

"What are you smiling at, daddy?" asked Vivienne.

He hadn't realized he was. "Oh, nothing. How's Pulaski?"

Her cheeks reddened, and she laid the phone aside for the first time since she left the shower. "Well, daddy, it's funny you should ask..." She took his hand in hers, and spoke with unusual solemnity. "Because Nick just asked me to marry him."

"I'm not surprised, pumpkin. You're quite a catch. So, what are you gonna say?"

She tried to mask her glee, but Vivienne had no poker face. *"Ialreadysaidyes!"* she blurted out, and threw her arms around her father.

He hugged her back, patting her damp skin. He was thrilled for his daughter, undoubtedly, but more than anything, he felt relief. Ron's one concern was that the death of the shaman might have broken the love spell, but with this revelation, he knew beyond reasonable doubt this was not the case.

"That's wonderful," he said.

Vivienne kissed him on the cheek. Once, twice, ten times. "You're the greatest daddy in the world, you know that?" She kissed him again. "The best *ever!*"

"I did what any father would have done," he said, though it was a lie. He really *was* the greatest father in all the world. The wedding was going to cost him a fortune, of course, but he couldn't put a price on his only daughter's happiness. All in all, it had been a successful day. The love spell had worked, the contract was broken, and he had saved himself ten grand on paying the mercenaries due to a combination of the men's greed and Duke's lightning-fast trigger finger.

"I love you, pumpkin," he said, and patted her head,

unaware that back in Thailand, in the mysterious clearing in the jungle...

≈

...the fire still burned.

Crimson flames roared, flaring brightly enough to catch the attention of the occasional driver on the lonesome mountain road.

None stopped their vehicles, nor dared to call the fire department. Why would they? Anyone taking that road knew all too well who lived in the stilt-house in the clearing. And though it had been quiet for almost a decade — and rumors had circulated of the sorcerer's retirement, or possibly even death — not one passerby was willing to venture into the jungle to check.

Well, no one except Nattawut.

He had been on his way home from working in the pharmacy when he spotted the fire from his motorbike. Growing up in a nearby village, Nattawut's parents had warned him never to wander near the old man's property, nor to set foot in that part of the jungle. His mother had spoken of the man's use of Yaa Sang, and, like a dutiful son, he had done as asked.

He never believed it, though, for Nattawut was not a young man prone to superstition. Years of studying medicine had opened his eyes to the wonders of science, and through that, he found he could explain most of what his parents believed to be magic and the supernatural. Their poisons, their remedies, the strange lights they saw in the sky... all had rational explanations, as long as you cared to find out about them. If anything, Nattawut regarded their beliefs as damaging, not just to his community, but to Thai people in general. He didn't want the rest of the world to regard his countrymen as superstitious bumpkins, instead of the doctors and lawyers and poets and artists that he associated with.

So when he saw the old man's home was ablaze, he took the disused turnoff, parked his bike by the side of the road, and battled his way through unimaginably thick vegetation that scratched and tore at his clothing. He could smell the fire, even if he could no longer see the tall flames and smoke that initially drew his attention.

He shoved the branches aside, wishing he carried an axe or a machete like his father used to back in his farming days. Nattawut dimly recalled following his father one time, tracking him through the jungle all the way to the house in the clearing, and watching as an old man with long, gray hair greeted him like a beloved acquaintance. He never asked his dad what the purpose of the visit was, and the time for that had long since passed, for his father had been dead fifteen years this April. What he *did* remember was the family suddenly coming into money a couple of weeks later thanks to the death of Nattawut's uncle, and his mother crying for days on end.

He paused to catch his breath, and heard the crackle of flames through the surprising calm of the jungle.

Not far now!

Pushing away from a tree, he resumed his journey. No one could have survived the blaze in the time it took him to reach it, but hopefully the old man and his daughter had made it out.

He could really smell it now. Not only burning wood, but meat, too. The thought turned his stomach, and though it was selfish, he hoped he wouldn't be the first to arrive on the scene. He did not want to have to dig the smoking bodies out of the ashes.

Light and fire splintered through gaps in the trees, casting hideous shadows that made the jungle feel not only alive, but angry. Nattawut increased his pace, arriving at last in the clearing, where the shack — or what remained of it — burned. The stilts had collapsed, and the roof had caved in, leaving a burning ball of immense heat surrounded by trees that appeared to be keeping their distance. Tiny golden embers wafted through the air like fireflies, before turning to snowy ash and spiraling out of existence.

Nattawut stood back, shielding his face from the inferno and helplessly watching the building crumble. The fire lit up the clearing, and he gazed around, searching for survivors and finding nothing but trees and a pond and a small wooden outhouse.

"I'm sorry," he said to no one. "I was too—"

The fire shifted.

At first, Nattawut thought the structure had collapsed further. He took a step closer, half-closing his eyes to protect them from the heat, and when he saw it — when he noticed what was emerging from the flames — his heart stopped beating for several seconds.

An arm, slim and blackened by fire, pierced through the charred remains. Nattawut stood, frozen in terror, as the rest of the impossible being followed, crashing through the crumbling structure and staggering free, a pitch-black nightmare backlit by fire like a demon from hell.

Falling to his knees, Nattawut clasped his hands and lowered his head. He prayed, closing his eyes as the violent hiss of the fire faded away to nothingness.

The delicate sizzle of boiling footsteps drew closer.

"Please," he whispered.

The demon approached.

"I have a family," he begged. "Spare me."

It stopped before him. He smelled its burning skin, and when the demon touched his chin and tilted his face towards its own foul countenance, he opened his eyes in acceptance of his fate. The damage the fire had done was shocking. The figure's cracked skin had been fried the deepest black, and a powerful amber light glowed between the myriad fissures that splintered the crispy layer of flesh.

"You," it said, and as it spoke, flakes peeled from its face. "Tell no one what you saw here today." The voice was lilting, melodic.

A woman's voice.

"No one," he said, struggling to form the words. "I promise I will tell no one."

The woman traced her fingers down his cheek as his body trembled. Nattawut stared at the ground, perilously close to delirium. And then... she walked away, her footsteps shimmering through the long grass.

"No one," he repeated. "I will tell no one."

And hours later, when the sun rose on the clearing, and the burning shack had been reduced to smoldering ashes, he was still there, on his knees in prayer. The hot rays scorched his skin, and he ran his fingers over his cheek. They came away with black soot on the tips. He wiped them clean in the dewy grass, and wept.

Death had touched him last night. It had touched him, and spoken to him, and he had lived to tell the tale.

But it was a tale he would never tell.

Ever.

For he had made the demon a promise.

"There are two rules in life," he remembered his father telling him, as they sat by a campfire watching the flames dance. He had been a teenager then, his father a grown man. "One, is that a man should always keep his promises."

Nattawut had nodded. That made sense. Keeping promises was important. "And what about rule number two?" he asked innocently.

His father had shivered. "Son," he had said, and put his hand on Nattawut's shoulder. "Rule number two is that you must never, *ever* fuck with a sorceress."

Shocked, Young Nattawut had promised he wouldn't... and he never broke his promises.

PART II

THE FALLOUT

18

IN THE STERILE BOARDROOM ON THE FIFTIETH FLOOR OF JARVIS Tower, Ron stood at the head of the table before his highest-ranked employees in a tailored suit that hung looser than it should. Yet another restless night had robbed him of both his appetite and his enthusiasm, a fitful sleep plagued by feverish dreams of—

No. Now was not the time to think about it. He had a job to do.

"Good morning, ladies and gentlemen," he said, for unlike his predecessor Peter Greyfriar, who operated a strict 'no broads in the boardroom' policy, Ron actually employed two women in senior positions. This was, of course, due to DEI frameworks that insisted he hire a couple of token females, but Ron had circumvented the mandate by person-ally selecting the prettiest young ladies in the shortest skirts. The fact that the women worked harder and better than their male counterparts never failed to annoy him.

"It's been a big year for Jarvis Media," he said, addressing the room with little of his trademark flair. "Tumultuous, undeniably, but we've made impressive gains in the marketplace. The, uh, Warners deal went through, profits were up six percent in the last quarter, and perhaps most impressively, Hank finally fooled some poor sucker into marrying him."

The assembled group laughed at that, none louder than Hank himself, who punctuated his chortles with a cry of, "Hey, it's true! You got me there, Ron!"

Ron nodded, satisfied by the response to his joke. It calmed him. All these years, and he never tired of the syco-phancy. "Okay, okay, settle down," he said, holding his hands up. "We've got a lot to discuss."

Six months had elapsed since the visit to Thailand. For the first five, Ron had enjoyed the best sleeps of his life. Without the looming threat of the shaman claiming his daughter, and with Vivienne busying herself planning her upcoming wedding, his nights had passed untroubled by bad dreams and visions of imminent disaster.

Then, about a month ago, he started seeing them.

The worms.

At first, they were on the street, and he made a point of going out of his way to stomp on the vile creatures and grind their slimy bodies beneath his heel. Then, they started appearing in his favorite restaurants; on the floor, on the table, and even in his food. Was it any wonder he was losing weight?

In his limousine, the worms crawled from between the seats and festered inside the drinks cabinet. They wrapped themselves around the washroom faucets, lurked beneath his desk, and turned up in his shoes, which he worried would signal a full-scale invasion of his penthouse.

He could see one now, in the corner of the boardroom. A wriggling horror, curling and uncurling its bloated body.

Ron took a drink of water. He usually despised men who

drank during a presentation — a weak mouth meant a weak mind — but the sight of the invertebrate set him on edge. He didn't dare ask someone to get rid of it. What was the point?

No one else could see them.

Two weeks ago, in the middle of a meeting, he had spotted one in the boardroom and ordered Johnson to deal with the creature. Baffled, the man had asked Ron if he was joking. In the end, the obsequious prick had pretended to remove the worm by scooping up thin air with cupped hands while the embarrassed employees cast their eyes down upon the table, unwilling to make eye contact with their CEO.

After that, Ron kept his observations to himself.

Was he working too hard?

Unlikely. He had always thrived on pressure, and gorged himself on risk. Nothing flustered him... so why did the sight of those fucking infernal worms make him want to tear out his hair and run screaming from the room?

Someone at the table cleared their throat.

Shit, how long had he been standing in silence?

"So..."

But all he could think about was the worm on the floor. A couple of his employees twisted their heads around to see what he was staring at.

Quick, say something.

His mind was blank.

Say anything!

The first phrase that popped into his head was, "Who, uhh, saw the game last night?"

"What game, Ron?" That was Frank Kerwin. Ron didn't like the man, and made a mental note never to promote him.

"The game," he muttered angrily. "Ah, forget it."

There were two worms now, right next to each other. Ron had recently read on the internet that if you cut a worm in two, both parts lived on. Was that true? He felt himself sweat.

"You okay?" asked Ruby Appleby, one of his female employees, a blonde with a peachy caboose.

"I'm fine," he snapped. "So, as I was saying... we've had a good year. A strong year. Winkleman will go over the slides with you later, because I'm not sitting through another one of his, umm..."

What word was he searching for? He took another drink. Someone coughed, and it was impossibly loud in the silence of the boardroom.

"Where was I? That's right, this upcoming year, we're looking to maximize growth in, uhh... foreign markets."

Gibberish. He was talking absolute gibberish, throwing out meaningless corporate buzzwords and hoping no one would notice.

He swore the worms were watching him.

"We need to collaboratively orchestrate cross-platform content," he said, watching in mounting horror as a third worm appeared from behind the others. "Uh, think *Netflix* meets *Prime,* people."

The underlings nodded appreciatively. "Great idea," one said.

"Stellar," said another. "I'll get marketing to draw up some slides."

"It's such a low-risk, high-yield idea," said a third. "That's some blue-sky thinking, Ron."

He couldn't hear them over the *slurp, slurp* of the worms as they slithered over each other in a grotesque knot. His hands tightened into fists, and he glanced at each employee, seeking validation and finding only confusion on their moronic faces.

Slurp, slurp.

"Umm, I need you to aggressively mesh," — he rubbed at his eyes — "cross-unit channels."

What the fuck did *that* mean? It didn't matter. His team nodded and smiled, and when one started clapping, the others joined in.

Slurp.

There was a whole pile of worms. Steam rose as their bodies squirmed together.

Ron placed his palms on the table. "Okay, that'll be all for today."

The people stopped clapping and stared at him in bewilderment. "I thought this was our half-year results?" said Kerwin. "Are... are we done here?"

More laughter, but not the good kind. Nervous chuckles, the kind that said, *hey, is the boss losing it?*

"I'm fine," he said, then realized no one had asked. "Just get out, okay?"

His dry lips smacked together, and he grabbed the glass and took a long drink. The refreshing liquid glugged down his throat, and—

Wait.

There was something in the water. It slipped down his esophagus and stuck halfway. He knew what it was. Ron didn't need a doctor to tell him there was a fucking *worm* in his fucking *throat.*

The glass fell from his hand and shattered, unleashing dozens of the repulsive beasts. Ron kicked them away, then turned to his employees. Aghast, they watched him, no one quite sure what to do.

"Meeting's adjourned," spluttered Ron, and he strode

from the room and barreled through the door into the corridor. "Uch," he hiccuped, in a fruitless attempt to dislodge the worm as he lumbered towards the washroom.

God, it tasted exactly how he remembered.

The washroom was empty apart from some asshole pissing at the urinal.

"Get out!" Ron roared, and when the man saw who was barking orders at him, he stuffed his junk back into his pants and ran from the room with a widening stain on his crotch.

Kicking open a stall door, Ron jabbed two fingers down his throat, fingering his tonsils until he retched. His stomach tightened, and up came his breakfast. The half-digested waffles unceremoniously hit the bowl, but still he felt the creature inside him. Screwing his eyes shut, he forced his fingers further, his shoulders jerking as his body reflexively rejected the intrusion.

With one final spasm, he heaved his guts into the toilet, ejecting the worm. It splashed into the bowl, wriggling amongst the vomit. Ron eyeballed the creature, then reached for the handle and flushed, watching the tiny monster disappear down the U-bend.

"Good riddance, motherfucker," he growled, then realized he was tough-talking a worm.

He exited the stall and drank from the faucet, then straightened his tie in the mirror. Unable to help it, his mind flashed back to that day in the Greyfriar building, and to that bag of thirteen worms he had dug up from the child's grave.

"It was worth it," he told himself. "It was *all* worth it."

He ran a hand through his thinning hair and closed his eyes, leaning on the basin. He was tired, that was all. In one month's time, he had a two-week vacation booked for Vivienne's wedding and honeymoon, and Christ did he need it. Once that was over, he could relax, having spent the previous twenty years worrying that his daughter would become the property of some wizard on her wedding day. At least he knew that was off the cards now.

The man was dead. Duke had killed him.

But what was it Suwin had said that fateful day in Thailand?

I won't let death stop me.

That bastard. He'd been trying to get into Ron's head, and he had succeeded. He supposed it was what the man did best.

Should've offered him a job, Ron thought, and smiled. *Maybe then you coulda banged his daughter.*

Feeling better — thinking about sex always improved his mood — Ron looked at his reflection, checking his hair and wiping the spittle that ran down his chin. The stall behind him opened, and he began washing his hands.

The door groaned on tired hinges, and Ron glanced up as — *clang* — it hit the wall. No one exited.

The stall was empty.

He looked over his shoulder, shrugged, and turned back to the mirror, where two hideously burned arms were reaching around him, one over his right shoulder and one around his waist. They gripped his skin, the talon-like nails tearing his shirt and digging into his flesh. He put his hands on them and felt intense heat rising from the groping limbs. The skin on his palms burned and spat, as over his shoulder appeared a head, black and charred and flaking, bright orange light escaping from between the swarming cracks in its miserable flesh. The mouth opened into a sneer, displaying perfectly white teeth and a pink tongue that flicked out across—

"*Fuuuck!*" screamed Ron.

He staggered backwards, slipping on the wet floor and falling heavily onto his ass, slapping madly at the arms of the dead person that... that...

But there *were* no arms around him.

Not anymore.

He was simply a sixty-year-old man lying on a washroom floor in an expensive suit, pummeling his own arms and chest with feeble, frightened blows. He lay there a moment longer, then scrambled gracelessly to his feet, afraid someone would come in and find him on the floor like a... like a fucking *worm*.

Turning his back on the mirrors, he brushed himself off.

Why? Think the shaman's ghost is coming to get you?

He chuckled to himself, but the hollow laughter failed to mask the truth in his dark, withered heart.

Because, in actual fact, that was *precisely* what he had thought was happening.

And frankly, the idea scared the shit out of him.

19

Neville Woods was drunk and horny as he cruised the bustling streets of Bangkok, the terrible burden of cash weighing heavily in his pocket. He had recently been paid for teaching a lesson to a street-punk who thought he could muscle in on another drug dealer's turf, and now he was looking to spend his earnings before he accidentally did something sensible. Luckily, the Australian, who had moved to Thailand fifteen years ago, knew precisely where he needed to go.

Madame Wang's Go-Go Bar.

Beneath pulsing neon signs that scorched his retinas, Woods strolled through Soi Cowboy, one of the city's busiest nightlife districts. Soi Cowboy was a sex tourist paradise, as alongside western staples like McDonald's and Subway were dozens of nightclubs and go-go bars. Beautiful young girls lounged on the street in lingerie and skimpy swimwear, aggressively beckoning him inside and waving price lists in front of his face, while slack-jawed tourists gawked and snapped surreptitious photos on their phones.

The booming sex trade was why Woods had moved here

in the first place. And if he happened to have become a mercenary-for-hire along the way, well, such was life. There was always room for a tough *farang* in Thailand, and while some ex-pats took jobs in the tourism industry, and others worked as fisherman, Woods broke people's arms and legs for money.

A job was a job, much like it was for the girls in Madame Wang's.

He preferred the go-go bars to the karaoke joints and the street-hustling freelancers. Sure, the girls were older than his usual tastes — sometimes as old as twenty-two — but they were better looking, and he got to watch them dance for a while as he made his selection. Woods, who considered himself a cultured man, enjoyed watching the girls shake their little bums. It was like going to the ballet, but for perverts.

Inside Madame Wang's, he ordered a drink and took his usual seat by the podium in the middle of the room, where eight girls gyrated their hips for the eager clientele. One initially caught his eye; a sweet young thing in a sparkling gold bikini that sashayed in all the right places. But the more he studied her clumsy, amateurish movements, the more he decided she would be a lousy lay. However, the girl beside her in the leopard print thong swayed confidently in a manner that suggested she knew *exactly* what she was doing. In order of importance, he checked out her arse and legs, then her tits, and, lastly, her face.

Satisfied he had made the right choice, Woods smiled at her, and she stepped down from the podium in five-inch heels and took a seat at his table. He knew the score — this was most assuredly *not* his first time — so he bought her a couple of 'lady drinks', as was the custom, and engaged in flirtatious small talk. After agreeing on a price, he slipped his arm around her slim waist and they headed upstairs through the beaded curtain.

Thumping bass bled through the walls, almost enough to mask the moans and grunts coming from the rooms they passed. The girl opened a door for him, and he smacked her arse and pushed her inside.

The barely furnished room was lit by a dim red light-bulb, and cooled only by a dust-caked electric fan that whirred sadly in the corner. Strewth, the fun hadn't even begun, and already he was too hot. Woods stripped his sticky, sweat-soaked vest off and the girl cooed sweetly, as if he was the first muscular Aussie she had ever brought upstairs.

He shoved her backwards onto the bed and playfully pounced on her. "Gotcha!" he cried, and spread the girl's legs, kissing her pussy through the thin strip of fabric. She giggled coyly as he worked his way up her body, tonguing her bellybutton and burying his face between her tits. And when she clamped her thighs around his waist and pulled him close, he suddenly realized why he had picked this particular girl over the others. It wasn't just because of her perky tits, though they had certainly played a part.

It was because she reminded him of the sorceress.

Crikey, he hadn't thought of *that* chick in a while. How he wished he'd fucked her, instead of coming in his own strides like some pathetic teenager. He wondered if she had *made* that happen using a magic spell, costing him his one chance at experiencing the pure sexual bliss of fucking a sorceress.

Still, he could always pretend. Woods may have been a violent thug, but he was a violent thug with a *vivid* imagination.

"Hey, you know black magic?" he asked the girl.

"Of course."

He smiled. The girl was a professional, and knew to agree with everything he said.

"Yeah? You cast a love spell on me?"

"Of course!" she repeated. "I make you love me *all night.*"

"Yeah, well, two hours maybe," Woods shrugged, and slid the leopard print thong down her long legs. "Jesus, you're a fucking beaut', ain't ya?" He sniffed the gusset of her thong, breathing in her scent, and tossed the flimsy under-garments to the floor.

The girl unbuckled his pants, smiling up at him as she did so.

"Yeah, you're a fucking sorceress, alright," he murmured as he fingered her pussy. "You're a sexy little witch!"

She tugged his pants and underwear down, gasping theatrically at the size of his stiff member. Woods assumed she did that for everyone, but it took nothing away from the thrill.

"Little witch," he mumbled, as he roughly entered her. He grabbed her arse with both hands and squeezed. "You like my magic wand, eh? You fuckin' like it?"

"Oh, I love it!" she said, and pumped her hips against him. She was good, he'd give her that. Damn good. He wondered if this was what it would have been like with the sorceress? He fumbled behind her back, unfastening her bra and freeing her tits, before placing his hands on the fleshy mounds and craning his neck up to the ceiling.

"That's it," he said, closing his eyes and picturing the sorceress's impossibly beautiful face. "Ride my broomstick, witch! Ride it!"

"Oh, so good!" she cried out. "Number one!"

Woods gasped in pleasure at the tingling sensation on his cock. It was as if dozens of tiny fingers were gently massaging his erection. "You *are* a fucking sorceress, you sexy—"

Oops.

Maybe he went a little too hard there, for he felt a tight pinch. He paused to readjust himself, and that was when the agonizing pain shot through his body, starting from his groin and working its way through his bloodstream with shocking speed.

"What the hell is that?" he asked, before the violent sensation rippled through him a second time, his mouth open in a silent scream.

"What's wrong?" asked the girl.

Woods couldn't answer. Gingerly, he pulled out of her, gazing down at the girl's vagina as his wet cock slipped free.

His eyes widened in fear.

"Oh, Jesus fucking *Christ!*"

Two scorpions crawled along his dick. One scuttled towards his thick nest of pubic hair, while the other clung on by its tail, the stinger embedded in Woods's meaty shaft.

The girl took one look at his penis and shrieked.

"You did this!" Woods shouted at her, staggering backwards on legs that were already numbing, waves of poison flooding his veins.

"Not me!" she said, throwing herself off the bed and scurrying, naked and screaming, from the room.

He backhanded his cock, knocking one of the scorpions loose. The other was stuck fast. Pinching the creature, he pulled, his foreskin stretching further than it ought to.

"Get off!" he cried. The room spun. He stumbled, collapsing backwards and sliding down the wall to a sitting position.

"Whaa tha fuuu...?"

He tried to raise one brawny arm and found he couldn't.

His head slumped forwards. He could breathe, and move his eyes, but other than that, the venom had paralysed him.

In his periphery, the shadows stirred.

The darkness seemed to come to life, amber trails swirling through the air and forming the shape of a human.

If Woods could have screamed, he would have rocked the entire building, for what came stalking towards him had no business being here.

Shit, it had no business being *alive*.

The Australian was afraid.

Good.

Anong wanted him to experience the terror of death, a feeling he had doled out on so many others.

Including herself.

She kneeled before him. Her profane glow lit up his sallow face. That night in the clearing, he had wanted her. And he would have taken her by force had the men not run out of time.

Time.

Men like him were always concerned with time. They never stopped to appreciate life. To them, time was money, and money was power, and *power* was life.

Power was what they prized above all.

Unable even to blink, the man gazed impotently at her. Where was his power now? Without his gun, and without his cock, he was nothing. Still, for the first time in his miserable, wasted life, he would prove useful.

From a small sack, Anong produced a handcrafted blade as sharp as a medical scalpel. She held it before him long enough for the man to understand the pain he was about to endure, then got to work. He was already naked, which saved her some time, and with careful fingers, she methodically carved symbols into his pliant flesh. She started from the soles of his feet and worked her way up, as, otherwise, the blood flowing down his body would only make her job more difficult.

When she saw the agony in his eyes, she cut a little deeper. A nick here, a cut there, shallow slices deftly parting his skin as, one-by-one, she carved the intricate runes. Their meanings evaded her — the writing predated even the Shang dynasty oracle bones — but unlike her father, who had spent years attempting to decipher the runes, Anong intuitively knew how to use them.

It was her gift, and her curse.

Blood gushed from the man's body, and she increased her pace. Tonight was a full moon, and if she missed her chance, she'd have to keep him alive for another month. The symbols covered his legs, his torso, his arms... even his penis. She sliced into his chin, beginning work on the face.

Almost ready.

A wheezing rattle escaped the man's lips. Yet despite the untold torment he endured, the symbols kept him alive. He needed to be, for the ritual to work.

Anong reached into the sack and lifted a nine-inch-long nail doused in toad venom. She held the nail above the man's head, the tip nestling against his scalp, and violently jerked downwards, cracking his skull like an icy lake.

The man's eyes flooded.

It was a little late for tears, but she was pleased to see them. Holding a bowl fashioned from the pulped leaves of a bodhi tree under his chin, she tilted his head, letting the teardrops weep into the waiting receptacle.

All that remained was the final step.

After the fire, Anong had retreated to the mountains for several months. There, she spent the days collecting ingredients, and the nights familiarizing herself with her unasked-for gifts. Her whole life she had denied them, but now there was no escaping her destiny. If she was born a sorceress, then a sorceress she would be. And those who had wronged her would fall, one-after-another, until none remained.

The man's tears dotted the bowl, and, with savage ferocity, Anong rammed the nail fully through his cranium.

His eyes bulged as the metal spike penetrated his brain. The first spots of blood bubbled to the surface, increasing in intensity until they gushed down his face. Anong placed her palm against the nail and shoved it all the way in. The body jerked and stiffened, blood spurting from the wound and flowing into the bowl from his mouth like a fresh mountain spring.

She mumbled ancient incantations in the same dead language she had scratched onto his skin, the bowl filling as the man's face grew paler, bloody tears streaking his gaunt cheeks.

Once the flow slowed to a trickle, Anong removed the container and placed it aside, the blood sloshing back and forth.

The man, who had suffered the trauma of a thousand deaths, was gone.

He would be the first of many.

For as Anong brought the bowl to her lips and drank, she visualized those who had destroyed her family and sent her father to hell.

Their day of reckoning fast approached... and none would live to tell the tale.

20

In the penthouse suite, Vivienne reclined by the window with an iPad in her hand, scrolling through a list of names in increasing agitation.

"Austin Swift?" she spat. "Is that a joke? I asked for *Taylor* to be invited, not him."

"She's on tour," came Nick's muffled reply.

Vivienne moved the tablet aside and looked down at her fiancé. His face was tucked between her legs, his unkempt hair brushing her thighs as he flicked his tongue over her vulva in a slobbering attempt to relocate her clitoris.

"Nick, honey," she said, guiding his head into position. "Don't talk with your mouth full."

She returned her attention to the iPad. Choosing guests for her wedding was proving more difficult than she'd imagined. Selena Gomez, Katy Perry, and Kendall Jenner had already turned the event down, but at least Glen Powell and Olivia Jade had confirmed their attendance, albeit for a sizeable fee.

"Logan Paul can make it, but Jake can't," she said, and shrugged. "That's fine."

"Mhmm," agreed Nick.

"And daddy wants Elton John to sing at it, but he's some old guy. I keep telling him, *he* might be paying for it, but it's still *my* wedding."

"Ahhhn maahhhhn."

She glanced at the face sandwiched between her thighs. "That's right, baby. And yours."

She looked at the screen again. So many names, so many guests. It was giving her a headache. She laid the tablet down and gazed out the window at the tiny ant-people scrambling about their dull, useless lives. Some people said money couldn't buy happiness, but those idiots were penniless yokels. Every one of them would trade places with her in a heartbeat. Who wouldn't want to sip champagne while a handsome movie star ate their pussy at ten in the morning?

A quiet knock at the door drew her attention away from the view.

"Come in," she said, watching the door open with a mischievous grin on her face.

Perlah, their Filipino maid, entered, and gasped in shock at the carnal display. She always did, and her expression of horror never failed to tickle Vivienne. Perlah half-turned away, looking anywhere but at Vivienne and Nick.

"The, uh, wedding planner is here," she said, her cheeks coloring.

"Perfect. Tell her I'll be there soon."

Seconds later, she realized she should have said, *tell her I'm just coming,* but Perlah had already left the room, and the moment had passed. Sighing, Vivienne pushed Nick's head back, placed her feet on his chest, and kicked him away. He fell backwards, staring up at her like an eager puppy.

"Did I do it wrong?" he asked. "I'm sorry. I can try again. I'll do it right, I promise."

"Jesus, you're so needy." She rolled her eyes and walked to where her fluffiest pink robe hung, slipping it on. Nick was on his knees, his cock stiff, his naked body a coiled spring of muscle. She doubted she'd ever tire of looking at it, but right now she needed some space.

"Go work out for a while," she said. "The camera adds ten pounds, and there's gonna be hundreds of them at our wedding."

He nodded enthusiastically. "Okay. I'll make you proud."

"I'd rather you made me come, but whatever." She waved him away. "What are you waiting for? Go! Shoo!"

Nick got to his feet and dashed obediently from the room. Vivienne watched his tight ass as he did so.

"What a fucking loser," she said, and opened a pack of Ozempic that was sitting on the breakfast bar. It was funny how things worked out. She thought she had wanted him back because she loved him. With a gun to her head, she would have *sworn* that was the case. But now, with Nick by her side twenty-four-seven, she understood her motivation better.

It was revenge.

Revenge on Nick for leaving her, and revenge on that slut Carol for stealing him away. It was as simple as that. The big Hollywood star who thought he was so great had, at Vivienne's urging, abandoned his career and walked away from a deal that would have cast him opposite Keanu Reeves to be her live-in *fuck toy*. It was almost too funny. Sure, he could be a real pain-in-the-butt sometimes, and she practically had to have him surgically removed from her just so she could go to the bathroom alone, but she had already decided she was gonna marry him anyway.

He was undeniably gorgeous, and they looked stunning together in photographs, and really, wasn't *that* what mattered in a marriage? And if not, well... she could always get Glen Powell's number at the wedding.

21

STAN DUKE HAD JUST STUFFED A CHUNKY WEDGE OF STEAK IN his mouth when his boss called. Without a second thought, he spat the meat onto his plate and answered. When Ron phoned, you didn't keep him waiting, unless you were keen to receive an earful of verbal abuse.

"Duke speaking."

A moment's silence followed, which struck him as unusual.

"*Stan... how are you?*"

And pleasantries? *Most* unusual.

"Is everything okay?" Duke reached for his wallet in case he needed to pay and run. "Where are you?"

"*I'm at home, and I'm fine.*"

"Glad to hear it." He wasn't sure he believed him. "What can I do for you?"

That silence again. Ron Jarvis was many things, but he was not quiet.

"*Well, like I already asked... I was wondering how you were?*"

The question caught Duke off-guard. In twenty-something years, his boss had never once asked him how he was.

"Yeah, I'm good, Ron. Having lunch at Corky's. They've got this new outdoor seating area, and—"

"*Shut up, Duke. This isn't a social call. I'm asking... purely out of interest, you understand... if you've seen anything odd lately.*"

"Anything odd?"

"*Yeah, y'know. Anything out of the ordinary.*"

Thrown by Ron's faltering delivery, Duke considered the query. "Well, now you mention it, I did see a woman this morning taking her dogs for a walk in a baby stroller. They were two of those pug dogs, you know the kind. One of them was wearing a top hat."

"*What the fuck are you talking about?*"

"Pugs," said Duke. "You asked if I saw anything unusual, and these dogs were in a stroller. Can you believe it? LA, man. This place is crazy." He cut a piece of steak. "Ron, you still there?"

"*I'm not talking about dogs, you fucking asshole. I mean... have you seen anything...*" — Ron sighed down the phone — "*...inexplicable?*"

"I can't say I have," Duke lied. "How about you?"

"*I'd rather not talk about it over the phone. Come see me, now.*"

"Sure thing," he said, but Ron had already hung up.

He took a last bite of the steak and left the money and a healthy tip on the table. Ron sounded spooked, and he wondered if he, too, had seen her.

The shaman's daughter.

Duke had first noticed her two days ago. Standing in the middle of the freeway with cars whizzing past her on either side, she was hard to miss. Then, yesterday, he had caught the reflection of her red and gold dress in the brushed metal walls of the Jarvis Tower elevator. He knew he should have told Ron, but he was ashamed to admit that, riding the elevator alone, he had been too scared to turn around, even when he felt a hair being plucked from his head.

That dress... it was the same one she had been wearing the night they murdered her.

And they *had* murdered her, hadn't they?

That was another reason not to tell Ron. A damn good reason. Because Ron had given Duke one job, and if he had failed in that simple task, well... there would be consequences.

Shit.

His current best-case scenario was that paranoia was causing him to see things. The girl was an illusion, a stress-induced hallucination.

"You hear me?" he shouted at the woman on the other side of the street, the one in the red and gold dress who watched him expressionlessly, the passers-by seemingly oblivious to her presence. "You're not real!"

He got in his car and started the engine. He noticed his leg was trembling.

"You're not fucking *real.*"

———

22

NICK PULASKI STOOD BY THE ARM EXTENSION MACHINE IN THE private gym on the ninety-eighth floor, staring at his nude reflection in the mirrors that lined the wall. He struck a pose like Arnie in his bodybuilding days, admiring his toned physique, his powerful arms, and his rippling, muscular stomach. He pivoted, looking back over his shoulder. As his gay fans often told him on social media, he looked even better from behind.

Yeah, well, Vivienne said you look flabby, so stop staring at your own ass and get to work.

The voice in his head was right. It always was. He and Vivienne were to be wed in one month, and her happiness was of paramount importance.

Paramount.

He chuckled to himself as he pulled on his shorts and began his warmup stretches. To think he had walked away from that lucrative four-picture deal with Paramount! The studio head, Kevin Ketcher, had been fucking livid. But careers were secondary to love, weren't they? Everything was.

Love was, love is, and love shall be.

That's what Vivienne had tattooed on her ankle, anyway, and though Nick wasn't exactly sure what the phrase meant, it was printed on his lover's heavenly body, so he was convinced it was wise.

Wasn't he?

At times, secretly, he entertained doubts. Hadn't he grown up *desperate* to be a movie star? Hadn't that been his lifelong dream, and the reason he had moved to California in the first place, leaving—

He belched, and tasted sick in his throat.

Don't think about that. Picture Vivienne instead.

Great idea. He would do just that. But it was funny... he swore he used to think about things *other* than Vivienne. When he reached back into his cloudy memories, he remembered feelings, and ideas, and dreams, and surprisingly few of them regarded his fiancée, his darling, his one true love.

For instance, he briefly recalled watching Jean-Claude Van Damme in *Bloodsport* as a child, and the admiration he felt for the man igniting his desire to sculpt his body and master a martial art. He also remembered his sadness when saying goodbye to his mother at the airport on the day he left home to try his luck in Hollywood. And most of all, he thought he remembered intense feelings towards a woman named Carol.

The name sent a shiver down his spine.

Who was she? And what had become of her? Occasionally, she crept into his brain at night, but when he tried to remember her, a sickness seemed to grip him, a sickness that rattled his bones and constricted his throat.

Had she somehow stood between him and Vivienne?

Ah, Vivienne.

He smiled. Such perfection. His every waking moment was spent pondering how to make her happy, how to show her he cared, how best to tongue her asshole.

And yet... it didn't always feel right. She treated him badly—

You deserve it.

—and she spoke to him like dirt.

You are *dirt.*

She never considered his feelings—

Why should she? You're a fucking idiot.

—and sometimes, when he messed up, she hit him. Not like before, when she had stabbed him. But hard enough to sting, or bruise, or bleed him.

He didn't think Carol—

Don't say that name, don't you ever say that name.

—had ever done that.

She tried to, though. She fought back when you were—

The internal voice fell silent, as if it had said too much. What did it mean? Who *was* Carol?

Needing answers, Nick wandered over to his cell phone. Was it safe here? Other than Ron, Vivienne, and the cleaners, he was the only person with access to the gym, and neither of the Jarvis clan had set foot in here in all the time Nick had known them.

So, yes, for once, he was absolutely alone.

Turning his back on the security camera, he logged into Facebook for the first time in months, where he was greeted by the dreaded '99+' notifications symbol.

Ignoring them all, he hit the search button, and the first person to pop up — the last name he had searched, apparently — was Carol Malone. Could it be her? The mysterious woman from his memories?

He tapped her name and almost dropped the phone as a

wave of nausea washed over him. Her profile picture was of her and Nick in matching swimwear. She was kissing his cheek as he carried her, yet the sight of her turned his stomach. Struggling to grasp the device with his sweaty hands, and with a migraine gnawing at his temples, he scrolled past the image to a timeline full of comments from concerned friends and family.

Carol, call me. We're worried.

You not responding to DMs lol?

Just let us know you're safe, ok?

Miss u, hon. Please call.

On and on it went. So many people. She was tagged in a few 'Missing' posts, but the photographs made him want to smash her face, smash it, smash it to fucking pieces and—

He shut his phone down in frustration. Who *was* this woman? He needed to find out, because deep in the recesses of his brain, *good* memories lay dormant. Memories of Carol. They had slipped between the cracks, but every now and again, one bubbled to the surface. He had loved her, once. He was sure of it.

And she, in turn, had loved him back.

So why did the thought of her make him queasy? It wasn't natural, as if someone had hypnotized him. But who? Not Vivienne, obviously, because she loved him and would never, *ever* hurt him. But perhaps one of Vivienne's friends? He wondered if it was the work of that shady 'Glen Powell' character she was always talking about.

With a deep breath, he picked up his phone and tried Facebook again. He had to squint when photos of her appeared, but he couldn't help noticing he was in most of them, his arm around her, a smile beaming from his lips.

They looked like two people very much in love with each other.

"Who *are* you?"

Visions of Vivienne danced through his head. God, could he not stop thinking about her for five fucking seconds? There *had* been someone before Vivienne. He knew it now. He held the proof in his hands!

No, the voice piped up again. *It's always been Vivienne, and her alone.*

"That's not true." He punched his fist against his head as if trying to knock some sense into it. "There *was* someone else."

If he could only see Carol again, just *once,* then he was sure he'd remember.

"I can show you her, if that's what you desire."

At first, Nick ignored the voice, assuming it was the usual outspoken chatterbox in his head, the one that spoke of nothing but Vivienne and convinced him to leave the past behind. But when it came again, soft and sensuous, he knew it to be different.

"But only if you're prepared to confront your mistakes."

He glanced around the gym. The machines sat silent and unused beneath the industrial glare of the strip lights, the weights stacked neatly where they belonged.

He was alone.

"Who are you?" He glanced behind the bank of cross trainers. Then, quietly, he added, "And what are you doing in my head?"

"But I'm not in your head, Mr. Pulaski."

A gentle hand rested on his shoulder, and he spun to face the intruder. "Listen, I asked you..."

But there was no one there. He let the aborted question trail off, and touched his shoulder, convinced the lingering presence of her fingers remained.

"Over here, Mr. Pulaski."

This time he turned immediately.

A woman stood before him. She was dressed in traditional Thai clothing, a fact he knew from his years spent watching Tony Jaa and Panna Rittikrai action movies.

"My name is Anong," she said, "and I'm here to help you." She smiled thinly. "To offer you a last chance at redemption."

Nick was confused. Did he know an Anong? Was this another woman he had loved and forgotten? He wanted — no, *needed* — the voice in his head to tell him what to do, but it had fallen curiously silent.

"What do you mean?" he asked. "Do... do we know each other?"

"You don't know me," she said. "But I know everything about you." She tilted her head to the side. "And I know what you did to Carol."

"Who is she? I feel like I used to know her. Maybe I even..." — he swallowed hard, worried Vivienne could somehow hear him — "...loved her."

"You remember correctly. Carol was indeed your lover." The woman took a step closer. "And she died by your hand."

"No," said Nick uneasily. "I don't remember that. You're lying. I've never killed anyone."

"That's what the voice in your head wants you to believe. I know this, because my father — under duress, I must add — put that voice there. Vivienne Jarvis and her father *forced* him to cast a spell on you."

He wasn't sure how to respond to that outlandish claim. "A spell? Are you fucking joking?"

"That's correct. A spell so that you would love her, and *only* her."

"Bullshit. There's no such thing as spells."

"Are you sure?" She walked towards him. "So if I were to dim the spell, so to speak, you wouldn't feel any differently?"

"There's no such thing as spells," he repeated defiantly, though something inside him felt different, like the mist in his head was evaporating.

"Don't you think it's strange?" she asked.

"What is?"

"The way you're looking at me. You think I'm beautiful, don't you? You *want* me."

"What? No, I..."

"It's okay," she said. "Most men do. But ask yourself, when was the last time you looked at another woman and *desired* the touch of their hand?"

"This is bullshit," laughed Nick. The mysterious woman was talking in riddles. And yet... she had a point. For the previous six months, he had devoted himself exclusively to Vivienne. He simply couldn't comprehend the idea of being with another woman. Even in his wildest, most erotic fantasies, it was *always* Vivienne. But this woman... yes, he could imagine being with her.

He imagined it all too easily.

"I've dimmed the spell," she said. "And I can break it, too, if I choose. You're not like the others, which is why I'm going to give you — and only you, Mr. Pulaski — a second chance. I can wipe the slate clean, and you can begin anew, untroubled by your dark secrets. My father tried to hide your memories, to taint them." Her expression turned grim. *"I* can erase them. But you must face up to your actions. You must acknowledge your complicity in the death of your beloved."

What the hell was she talking about? What complicity?

"I told you," he said, turning away from her. "I've never killed anyone. I *couldn't* do it."

"And yet you did. Out of all the options available, you chose to—"

"I didn't fucking kill her!" he snapped. "Whoever the hell she is... or was." He glared at the woman. Her beauty paled in comparison to her cruelty. "You're a liar. A dirty, rotten liar."

"Perhaps words aren't enough," she said, as she moved closer. "Perhaps it would be easiest if you saw for yourself." She placed her hands on his temples. "Here, Mr. Pulaski. Let me remind you."

23

A DAM BROKE IN NICK'S BRAIN.

That's how it felt to him, anyway, like millions of gallons of memories and thoughts and feelings were flooding his synapses. He reached out for balance, but it was useless. As his legs gave way, he collapsed to the gym floor, clamping his fists over his eyes.

All at once, he remembered everything.

He remembered his childhood, his family, his friends.

He remembered his torrid relationship with Vivienne Jarvis, and how much he hated her.

He remembered Carol; from their early, tentative kisses and teenage fumbles in the backseat of his car, to their joy at being reunited all those years later, their love for each other as strong as ever.

And then, finally, he remembered — in graphic, unflinching detail — how he had pounded Carol's skull until it shattered, then dragged her corpse outside and set it alight. He hadn't just killed her, like the woman had claimed.

He had annihilated her.

"No! No! God, please, no!"

A lifetime of suppressed memories overwhelmed him. Curling into a fetal position, Nick sobbed, gripping handfuls of his hair. He tore out two thick tufts and stared up at the woman with manic eyes. *"What have you done to me?"*

"I broke the spell," she said. "Temporarily."

"There is no fucking spell!" Tears flowed down his cheeks. *"I didn't kill Carol! It's not true!"*

"Then tell me... do you love Vivienne Jarvis?"

"Of course not!" he roared.

Jumbled thoughts rampaged through his mind. He hated Vivienne... so what the fuck was he doing with his life? He was engaged to a selfish brat he couldn't stand, while his career and reputation lay in tatters. And as for...

"Carol," he whimpered.

Oh god, Carol.

Nick glared blearily up at her. "You did this."

"No. My father. A gifted sorcerer."

"He did this to me?" Nick took a breath, and began to rise, his limbs trembling in fury. *"He* made me kill Carol?"

"No. My father may have cast the spell, but *you* are responsible for your actions, Mr. Pulaski. You embraced its dark potential."

"No. I'd never hurt her. You fucked with my head."

"The spell was two-fold," the woman replied, unshaken by his simmering anger. "You would fall in love with one woman, and be repelled by another. But that was all. You could have simply left Carol. You could have moved out, or asked her to leave. But you didn't. *You* chose violence, Mr. Pulaski. It was *you* who chose murder."

Nick staggered to his feet. He stood a full twelve inches taller than the woman. "Bullshit. You made me do it. I remember now. You forced me." He moved closer, his shadow falling over her pretty face, and grabbed her arm. "You ruined my—"

"*...Nick?...*"

He froze.

That voice...

It couldn't be.

"*...Nick, is that you?...*"

It was coming from behind.

His grip on the woman loosened. When he released her, he noticed the red marks his fingers had left on her arm.

"Turn around," the woman said. "Turn and face your lover."

But he was afraid. To look at Carol, to see her again after what he'd done...

"No," he said. "It wasn't me." He clenched his fists, his mind clouding with anger. "It was *her*, Carol. She did this to me. This fucking witch."

"*...Look at me, Nick...*"

"No. It's a trick." He placed his hands around the witch's throat. She neither struggled nor fought back, not even as he closed his eyes and tightened his grip. "Make it stop! You hear me? Make it—"

Nick screamed as his hands burned. He opened his eyes, and there, where seconds before had stood the witch... was Carol.

"Oh *Christ*," he said, taking a horrified step backwards. The abominable nightmare stood before him like an atrocity risen from the tomb.

"*I'm so warm, Nick,*" she said. "*I'm burning up.*"

She had no face. Where it should have been hung a limp sack of smashed bone that draped across her burned and mutilated breasts. The flaccid balloon of flesh shifted as she spoke, as if somehow, amongst the carnage of scorched tissue, there still existed a mouth.

"Go to her," the witch said. She was behind him now. "Go to your lover and explain why you did this to her."

"I didn't do it," said Nick. He looked at the blackened, foul thing. It was fried to a crisp, the broken limbs jutting out at odd angles. "They put a spell on me!" He pointed towards the witch's passive face. "It was her, understand? She fucking made me do it!"

"Why, Nick? Why did you hurt me?"

"I didn't, I swear!"

"I thought you loved me."

"I didn't fucking kill you! They made me! They fucking forced me to do it!"

"That's not true, Nick. I saw it in your eyes."

He turned to the woman. "Tell her! Tell her you cast a fucking spell on me!"

"She knows. We've had a good talk, Carol and I. All she wants is an apology."

"I've nothing to apologize for, you cunt!" He spun, facing Carol's charred, crushed remains once more. "Carol, you have to believe me. I would *never* hurt you. I wasn't myself, okay? I wasn't in control. I—"

Wait... what was that in her hands?

What was she holding?

She lumbered closer. *"It wasn't just me, Nick."*

"Good god," he said, as his gaze fell upon the tiny, rotten creature clasped in her hands. The sac-like mass throbbed.

"This was going to be our baby."

The delicate flap of skin that hung from her neck rose up as if buffeted by wind, swaying unsteadily and revealing the full horror of her pulped face. The splatted, dribbling eyeballs, the flattened nose, the broken teeth that dropped to the floor. She raised the bloody embryo higher, offering it to him.

"*Meet... your son.*"

"That's not mine!" he screamed, as he snatched the unborn monstrosity from her hands and hurled it to the ground with a juicy splat. "Make it stop!" he cried, turning to the witch. He fell to his knees. "Please! Make it stop! Make me forget again!"

"You would choose blind allegiance to Vivienne Jarvis over facing your past mistakes?" asked the witch. "Over owning up to them?" She leaned closer. "Over a simple apology?"

"Yes! Yes! I can't take it anymore! It wasn't my fault, I don't deserve this!" He was shrieking now, and battering his fists off the floor. It was all he could do to keep insanity at bay.

"You accept no responsibility for your actions?"

He stared up at her, the veins in his neck bulging. "*It wasn't my fucking fault!*"

"Such a strong body," the witch said sadly. "Such a fragile mind."

The burning hands clamped over his shoulders, and Nick screamed.

"*I didn't fucking do—*"

The mirror shattered. It exploded outwards in a deafening crash, thousands of shards of razor-edged glass raining over the wooden floor. The pieces skittered like insects, slicing Nick's skin and embedding themselves in his firm flesh. But the burning hands... they were gone.

They were *all* gone. The... the woman...? Wait, what woman? He rose on shaky legs, using a rowing machine for leverage, and glanced around the empty gym. His reflection stared back at him from the unbroken mirror, and he ran his hands over his arms, searching for cuts and stray glass, and finding none.

"Dreaming," he said to himself. "I was dreaming."

He smiled as the dying memories faded, receding into his subconscious, then further, deeper, forever out of reach.

"A nightmare," he whispered, thankful he couldn't remember the details. But wasn't that always the way with dreams and nightmares? They never lasted.

Even the good ones.

How the hell had he fallen asleep while working out? If Vivienne caught him, she'd be so mad! Thinking of her, he dropped to the floor and began his push-ups, determined to make her proud on their wedding day. As he watched himself in the mirror and started to count, he thought he saw two unusual marks on his shoulders. Like the dream, they were fading fast, and after the third push-up the impressions were gone entirely, but he could have sworn they looked like burns.

Burns in the shape of handprints.

"Nick, my man," he said with a chuckle, his mind empty once more. "You are seriously losing it."

24

VIVIENNE DIPPED HER TOES INTO THE BATHWATER AND nodded approvingly. The temperature was a perfect ninety-five degrees, which was good news for the maid. Unlike their previous one, who had been sacked for unauthorized adjustment of the thermostat, Perlah was smart enough to obey Vivienne's strict instructions, which was why the bathroom smelled of peaches, Alexa was playing David Guetta, and freshly laundered pink bath towels had been laid out in size order. Perlah had even lit eight candles and placed them around the perimeter of the room, circling the gold clawfoot bathtub that sat in the center. It was off-script, but, luckily for her, Vivienne approved.

Slipping out of her robe, she stepped into the tub, swooning down under the water until the mountainous frothy bubbles covered her breasts. She rested her arms on the sides and closed her eyes with a contented sigh.

Don't fall asleep in the bath, her maids used to say to her when she was a kid. *You'll drown!*

It was sage advice, but Vivienne had never listened to

others. She did what she wanted, and rarely, if ever, paid the cost.

That's what wealthy daddies are for, she thought, and giggled.

The water soothed her, and boy, did she need soothing. As usual, the wedding planner had brought nothing but problems. The venue was demanding payment, the DJ had been arrested in Malaysia for drug trafficking, and the flowers she had requested did not actually exist. According to the unhelpful planner, the biollante flower — which some troll online had recommended to her — was from a Japanese monster movie. Problems, problems, problems, and never any solutions.

"Fucking stupid cunt. What the hell is daddy paying her for?"

She relaxed into the water, the bubbles tickling her chin. Something brushed past her feet. A sponge? It didn't matter, it was gone now. She briefly entertained the idea of finishing herself off after Nick had failed to do so, but she was too tired.

Planning a wedding was hard work.

Who knew?

Her phone vibrated on the wooden table beside the tub. God, could she not get two seconds of peace? It was probably the planner, or one of the Jonas Brothers begging for an invite to the wedding. Well, fuck that. She ignored the vibrations and let the phone ring out.

The sponge touched her toes again, and she squirmed. Perlah must have left something floating in the water.

"That dumb bitch," she grumbled, and leaned forward, spreading the bubbles apart above her legs. There was definitely *something* here, but she'd be damned if—

Then she saw them.

The hands.

"Oh shit," she whispered, as the fingers wrapped themselves around her ankles and locked into place. She tried to stand, but the ghoulish hands yanked her under the water.

Vivienne chose the wrong moment to scream.

Bathwater flooded her mouth, and she choked, thrashing her arms. A numbing sensation in her legs pulsed through her body, her limbs falling limp and splashing into the water, where they floated lifelessly.

Panicking, she tried in vain to raise her head above the surface.

It was no use.

She couldn't move.

And there Vivienne lay, as, through the ripples, she saw a figure rising from the water.

Oh god, oh god.

It dragged itself out of the tub and loomed over her, the distortions of the water lending the dark-haired, yellow-clad figure a twisted funhouse appearance. The figure bent over, taking Vivienne by the hair and lifting her head until, at last, it broke the surface.

Vivienne choked, spluttering a lungful of water into the tub, and gazed up into the eyes of Anong, the shaman's daughter.

She was soaked, her black hair clinging to her face, her yellow dress tight and semi-transparent. Before Vivienne had a chance to scream, the witch released her, and she plunged back underwater, powerless to stop herself. This time, she kept her mouth closed, trying not to breathe. Seconds ticked by, but they felt like hours. The witch lifted Vivienne's head again.

"You fucking bitch!" Vivienne screamed. "You whore!"

"And the same to you," smiled the witch.

Vivienne once more slipped below the surface. She lay still, drawing on her pilates breathing training. She relaxed her mind, entering a state of bliss, letting the—

"Blaaaaaaargh!"

Her scream opened the floodgates. More bathwater poured down her throat as the witch pressed her knee down on Vivienne's stomach.

Please stop! she wanted to yell, but it came out as a gargled nothingness. *Let me up!*

She couldn't breathe... shit, she couldn't fucking *breathe!* Why wouldn't the witch let her up? Was she planning on killing her? Dark shadows closed in around her, and then, as her life began to ebb away, she felt cool air on her nose.

The water level was dropping.

It reached her mouth, continuing to drop, lower and lower until Vivienne lay damp and naked and choking in the empty tub.

The witch sat atop her.

"You bitch," sobbed Vivienne. With no power in her neck, her head drooped to the side, and she half-spat, half-vomited the remaining liquid. "No one treats me like this. I'll fucking kill you."

"You're in no position to say that."

The bitch had a point. All Vivienne could do was scream, and what use was that?

"What have you done to me?" she asked through angry tears, as she stared at the side of the tub.

"Nothing compared to what your family did to mine."

"What are you talking about? We didn't do anything!"

"My father is dead," said Anong.

"So what?"

"Your father had him killed."

Ah.

At last, Vivienne understood. Though she had been unaware of the hit — she *had* just gotten engaged, after all — it did not surprise her to learn her father had killed the old wizard. Under the circumstances, she would have done the same.

"They tried to kill me, too," the witch said. She turned Vivienne's head towards her, then bunched her dress in her hands and lifted it, raising the garment far enough to reveal the grotesque wound to the left of her bellybutton.

"Ew, that's gross," said Vivienne. "You should get that looked at."

"That's where they raped me."

Vivienne tried to shrug. "Okay. But what the fuck do you want *me* to do about it? I wasn't even there! I had nothing to do with this!"

The witch let her dress fall back into place. "At the very least, I expected an invitation to your wedding."

Was this cunt serious? She stared into the woman's eyes, and decided that yes, she most certainly was. "I... I don't have your address. Like, do you even have postal workers in the jungle?"

"My address. Of course, how foolish of me." Anong held her hand out and extended the index finger. The nail grew before Vivienne's eyes, sharpening to a fine point. "Let me write it down for you."

Vivienne's heart pounded. Along with her mouth and eyes, it was the only part of her that still seemed to work. "It's okay, it doesn't matter," she said quickly. "You don't need an invitation. You can come."

"Verbal invitations aren't worth the paper they're written on," smiled Anong. "I expect a proper one from a woman of taste such as yourself. I want gold leaf and calligraphy and scented paper." She lowered her hand, the taloned finger pointing at the flesh of Vivienne's bare stomach. "And I'd accept nothing less."

"No, no, I told you. You're invited. Okay? *You're fucking invited!*"

"Stay still," said Anong. "This is going to hurt."

She jabbed her finger forwards.

Vivienne screamed as the nail penetrated her belly. Hot blood pumped from the wound and splattered on the gold ceramic tub.

"Stop! Please, stop! Don't do this to me, I told you, you're invited! You can even have a fucking *plus-one!*"

Anong's movements were precise, each one slicing open a shallow trench of skin.

"Don't!" cried Vivienne. "I'm begging you... please, get my — *ow!* — get my daddy, he'll pay — *ah, fuck!* — he'll pay you! He'll give you anything you — *ow fuck that fucking hurts so bad!*"

Her body jerked as the scratches grew more intense, and she lay there, defenseless, as the evil fucking witch hacked and slashed at her gorgeous, soft skin, skin that Chris Hemsworth had once described as 'creamy.' She thought of him then, and of her many lovers and conquests, trying to distract herself from the painful assault.

It didn't work.

She tried thinking of Nick, and how good he would look in his tuxedo, but that, too, was not enough. And so she dreamed of vengeance, and of turning the tables on this vile woman who lived in a jungle shack like a fucking primitive. She pictured herself hacking the woman's head off and tossing her body on a pyre. She imagined unleashing starving, feral hounds to rend her limb-from-limb. No, those fates would be over too quickly, and this woman deserved to suffer. Perhaps locked in a cell and forced to eat her own shit until she vomited up her guts? Or a chainsaw shoved right up her—

"All done," said Anong. She put her hands on Vivienne's wet, tear-streaked cheeks, and tilted her head up to see the damage the witch had wrought on her young body. Her stomach was a mass of scars and exposed, bloody tissue. "I will await my invitation."

"I'll kill you," breathed Vivienne. "I'll fucking *kill* you."

Anong's yellow dress was soaked in her blood. "So do it," she said, and leaned in *real* fucking close. "I'm right here."

Vivienne willed her body to move, to do what she asked of it. Nothing. She was as limp as a noodle. A fucking *noodle!*

"Thought not," said Anong. Contorting her body into position, she placed her face above the bloody mess of Vivienne's belly. Then, with aching slowness, she licked up the blood, lapping at it with her long, pink tongue, her eyes closed as if lost in ecstatic reverie.

Vivienne's useless head slumped to the side once more, the nightmare image of the woman drinking her blood mercifully out of view. "I'll kill you," she muttered, over and over. "I'll kill you. I'll kill you."

After a while — it could have been minutes, it could have been hours — her toes and the tips of her fingers started to tingle. The sensation worked its way through her limbs, life returning to her useless meat-sack of a body. When she felt strong enough, she raised her head. The witch was gone, the bathroom was empty, and her phone buzzed nearby. Using every last reserve of strength and willpower, Vivienne gripped the sides of the tub. The effort exhausted her, but she managed to haul herself up from the sticky pool of blood and snatch her phone from the side table with frail fingers. As she did, she looked down at her belly, at the words scored into her flesh. They were hard to read upside down, but Anong had told her it was an address.

An address for the wedding invitation.

Vivienne stabbed at the phone with her thumb, answering the call and leaving a bloody thumbprint on the screen.

And there, lying naked in the bath, and drenched in her own blood, she put the cell to her ear, choked back a sob, and screamed, *"Daaaaaaddddddy!"*

25

Ron, Stan Duke, and Vivienne sat in the Jarvis Tower security office before a bank of color monitors. Duke flicked through various channels on the center screen, checking each available feed. High-definition security cameras covered every square inch of corridor, yet with each click of the button, the monitor simply changed from one empty hallway to another.

There was no evidence of any intruder.

Ron chewed the end of a cigar. The only ways into the penthouse were by the private elevator and a staircase, both accessible only to those with a keycard. It was possible someone could have stolen or cloned a keycard, but there was no record on the system of anyone accessing either entryway.

He glanced at his daughter. "You sure you're okay, pumpkin?"

"I'm fine," she sulked, one hand tucked under her loose-fitting tee and scratching at her belly. Ron had never seen anything like it. By the time he and the on-site medic had arrived, the fresh wounds had stopped bleeding, and the cuts had healed into thin white scars that looked several weeks old. It was impossible, they all knew, and yet... a lot of impossible things had been happening lately.

"No trace of her," said Duke. "Not one goddam trace." He clicked the button again, revealing another vacant corridor. "Viv, are you sure you didn't—"

"Do it to myself? You fucking asshole. I told you, it was *her.*"

"What do you think about that, Duke?" asked Ron.

"It couldn't have been her," Duke protested, though the tremor in his voice betrayed him.

Ron pounced on the moment of weakness. "That's right," he said, locking eyes with his security chief. "It can't be Suwin's daughter, because you killed her, didn't you?"

"That's right. We shot her, dragged her body to the shack, and burned her and her old man up. No one could have survived."

"She told me you raped her," said Vivienne.

"What?" Duke's cheeks flushed. "No, not me. The other idiots did that, and anyway, she already got revenge on..."

The man trailed off, and Ron grabbed him by his shirt. "Finish that fucking sentence."

"Well, it's not like..."

"Not like *what,* Duke?"

The normally unflappable security chief looked flustered. "It was that guy your friend Edgar hired. He fucked her, and he was dead before we reached the truck. I figured she'd put a curse on him or something. But I saw her die, I swear to that. And anyway, if she wanted revenge, why wait six months? If she didn't harm me before, then if she *is* still alive, I think—"

"*If she's still alive?*" Ron glared at him. "You just told me she was fucking dead!"

"She is! She probably cast one of her spells right before—"

"Did you see her body?"

Duke fumbled a cigarette from the carton. "She was dead long before the mercenary finished fucking her, okay? She was absolutely—"

"Did you see her body *burn?*"

Struggling to spark his lighter, Duke took the deepest breath of his life. "No," he said in a measured tone. "I didn't see it burn all the way. But there was no way she could have dragged herself out of there."

"Jesus," said Ron.

"Look, even if she did survive, how did she get into Vivienne's bathroom?"

"I don't know, Duke. That's what I pay you for, isn't it? I mean, it sure as hell isn't for your skills as a hired killer."

Wounded, Duke resumed flicking through the channels.

But Ron wouldn't let it lie. This was his *daughter* they were talking about, for Christ's sake. "You sure you ain't seen anything funny lately? Anything weird? Because I sure have. I've been seeing all sorts of fucked-up shit from my past."

Duke licked his dry lips. "I've not seen anything."

Ron knew he was lying. He knew, because Duke never lied, and he was doing a poor job of it. "You saw what she did to my daughter, right? What she did to my Vivienne?"

"Yeah, I saw."

Ron snorted. "Show him again, pumpkin. Show him what she did to you."

"Come on, man," said Duke. "I already—"

Vivienne lifted her shirt. The words, so brutally scratched into her flesh, were plainly visible.

512 MESQUIT STREET

"You see that?" asked Ron. "That's because of you, Duke.

You and your fucking incompetence." He turned to Vivienne. "Okay, pumpkin, pull your shirt down. And don't worry, I know all the best surgeons. We can fix that in time for your honeymoon."

Vivienne looked at him incredulously. "But what if she comes back? What if she does it again?"

"She won't get the chance," he said. He lit his cigar. "The dumb broad gave us her address."

"You want me to pay her a visit?" asked Duke.

"I think you fucking better," said Ron. "Assemble a team. If she wants an invite that badly, then we should deliver it personally."

"I'm on it, boss," said Duke. He tapped at his phone, clearly sensing a way to atone for his stupidity.

"And this time," said Ron, "be a good little soldier, and make sure she's dead."

Vivienne gripped her father's arm. "Yeah... this time, bring me her fucking *head.*"

26

THE SUN HAD SET ON LOS ANGELES BY THE TIME THE BLACK transit van pulled up outside 512 Mesquit Street, a deserted warehouse in the city's wholesale district. The moon shimmered in the sky, the silence of the block broken only by the weary groan of the van doors opening.

Duke was first out. He checked for pedestrians or workers, and, as expected, found none. The area had been decimated by fire about a year ago, an out-of-control inferno that had gutted the street, killing fifteen and reducing the warehouses to dangerous, empty ruins. Not even the pimps or the dealers bothered coming out here now.

Duke fixed his black ski mask and signaled his men. Two of the most capable members of Ron's security squad, Singh and Lawson, exited the vehicle in matching tactical gear, each carrying a semi-automatic rifle. Duke, as a man who valued accuracy over power, preferred the comfort of the pistols strapped to his waist.

"This way," he said, and the pair followed him to the warehouse Anong had given as her address. Like most of the nearby buildings, the damage was severe. The walls were charred a deep black, and large portions of the roof were missing.

"She's hiding out in this dump?" asked Singh.

"Apparently so," Duke replied.

He looked back at the two men he had hand-picked for the mission. Would they be enough? He hoped so. Bringing more than two would have made him appear frightened, and Singh and Lawson were tough hombres who knew how to handle themselves. When, in the van, he had told them the target was a young Thai woman, they had laughed. Why the hell would it take three men to bring in one woman, Singh had asked. But when Duke informed him the target had scarred Ron Jarvis's daughter, the laughter died away. Jarvis paid his security team well, and an attack on Vivienne meant this was no ordinary assassination.

This was personal.

He had, of course, neglected to mention her use of black magic. Though it might appear a significant detail to an outsider, Duke doubted they'd believe him. And anyway, it didn't matter. Their orders were to shoot on sight, and shoot to kill. They wouldn't give her time to cast one of her spells. His only concern was that they were walking into a trap. The woman had willingly given them her address. Did she expect them *not* to pay her a visit?

"Be careful," he said, as they approached the boarded-up entrance. "She's wily. Place might be booby-trapped."

"It's one chick," said Singh. "You sound like we're taking on an army."

Duke grunted in response and peeled the boards from the entryway. Behind them was a door held shut by a flimsy chain and padlock. Two hard whacks from the butt of Lawson's rifle were enough to deal with it. The lock clunked to the ground, and Duke pushed the door open.

Moonlight flooded in through the broken roof and glistened off the fifty-foot high metal shelving units. A hypodermic needle crunched under Duke's feet as he entered. He drew both pistols as they traversed the main room, stepping over debris and searching for exits and pockets of darkness where Anong could be hiding.

A fire-ravaged steel staircase led to a gangway that circled the room. Duke signaled to Lawson to investigate the upper floor, while he and Singh took the lower level. Lawson nodded and stepped onto the staircase. It wobbled threateningly, then seemed to settle.

Christ, thought Duke. The whole place was a death trap. He turned to Singh and gestured to a doorway at the end of the room. Stealthily, they made their way towards it. Duke peered around the side into the pitch black corridor. A flashlight would destroy the element of surprise, but also help them avoid any nasty surprises, so Duke switched his on and shone it down the corridor. Paint peeled from the cracked ceiling, and murky green fluid leaked into puddles.

Singh turned his own flashlight in the opposite direction, the narrow beam picking out flame-scarred walls and a broken glass box where a fire axe used to hang.

Duke motioned for them to split up, and the two men went their separate ways. Hell, it was only one woman. Sorceress or not, he reasoned, *nobody* could argue with a bullet between the eyes.

Travis Lawson was a man who followed orders.

It was what he did best.

Not blessed with the most original mind, Lawson preferred to let others make his decisions for him. From his mother to his friends to his superiors in the military, he had discovered at an early age that doing what he was told was the safest course of action. If left to his own devices, he was prone to making blunders that often resulted in injury or death to those around him.

So when Duke — his boss for the last seven years — had instructed him to take the rickety stairs, Lawson did so without question. Duke was smart, and he probably had a good reason for sending Lawson up, rather than going himself. It was not his place to question orders, even if they put his life at risk. That was what he was paid to do; risk his life for others.

Lawson had no fear of dying; he had done it twice before. Once from an overdose, and once from having his skull split open by a machete-wielding lunatic. He had survived both, though he hadn't exactly come through unscathed. The machete had cleaved his face in two, and even if he could have afforded it, no amount of cosmetic surgery could have repaired the damage. The blade had shattered most of his front teeth and left an unseemly scar that ran from his hairline to his chin, splitting his nose and lips right down the middle.

Beauty is only skin deep, a man in a bar had once told him, seconds before Lawson beat the sarcastic bastard to a pulp with a pool cue. Bullshit. Since the attack, no woman had blessed him with more than a fleeting, horrified glance. Even the hookers rejected him. Lawson believed — in his more lucid moments — that if Stan Duke hadn't spotted his potential, he'd be in prison or dead. But Duke had given him a job, and turned Lawson's life around.

He owed the man everything.

The stairs creaked alarmingly with each cautious step. He noticed the bolts that held the staircase to the wall were loose, and in some cases, missing entirely. With no roof over this part of the building, the acidic LA rain had doubtlessly worked to erode the metal over time.

He quickened his pace until he reached the gangway. It felt more secure, and he was able to rest his weight without fear of the structure collapsing. The moon shone above him, so close he considered reaching out to touch it. He was up high, all right.

Real fuckin' high.

As he crept along the narrow walkway, Lawson paused occasionally to check for movement or signs of life down below. Nothing. He couldn't even see Duke or Singh anymore. Readying his weapon, he carried on, keeping close to the wall in case—

Wait. Something ahead.

Light from an unobstructed doorway. How had he not noticed before?

The light flickered. Candles? That would make sense. There was no power in here. He sidled along, gripping his rifle and dreaming about the bonus he might get for being the one who killed the woman.

Shoot on sight, and shoot to kill.

He would. Even though it was just one woman... he would shoot her, and kill her, and ask no questions. Those were his orders, and he would follow them as surely as night followed day.

The woman was singing. Her voice drifted, carried by the cold night wind. The song was pretty, though he didn't understand the words.

Shoot on sight.

So much caution for one little woman.

And shoot to kill.

What the hell was so dangerous about her? Why

couldn't they bring her in alive? He waited by the doorway and steeled himself. The candles cast her shadow on the wall, and he watched her hands work her hair loose, letting the strands fall across her shoulders.

Shoot on sight.

He wrapped his finger around the trigger.

And shoot to kill.

Shit, she was undressing. Her shadow casually shrugged her clothes to the floor, blissfully unaware of Lawson's lurking, deadly presence. Was it definitely her? It had to be. He would check first, though. To be sure.

With great care, Lawson peeked around the doorway. A woman stood with her back to him wearing nothing but panties. The candlelight played across her skin, yet other than a wooden bucket by her feet, she appeared to be standing amidst a black, hopeless void.

Is it her?

She bent over, stepping out of her underwear.

"Jesus," breathed Lawson.

Shoot on sight.

"Hold it right there," he said, rounding the corner. The woman gasped in shock and spun to face him. She made no effort to cover her nakedness.

"Who are you?" she asked.

And shoot to kill.

Lawson deselected the safety.

"I'm here to kill you," he said, inching closer.

Shoot on sight.

"Oh." She sounded disappointed. "Can it wait? I was about to bathe."

This confused Lawson. Why wasn't she afraid? Not just of the gun, but of his face?

His gaze traveled up her body.

And shoot to kill.

He raised his rifle, resting the sights over her chest.

"If you must kill me," she said, "at least help me wash up first. I'd like to die clean." She crouched beside the wide bucket and lifted a sodden sponge from the water. She ran it over her face, dabbing at her neck. "Won't you help me, Travis?"

Lawson lowered the gun. Had he told her his name? And more importantly, when was the last time a woman looked at him without screaming in terror?

"Please," she said. "It's not like I can do anything to you." She glanced down at herself. "I'm... I'm *naked.*" She said it as if he hadn't noticed.

Shoot on sight.

Why, though? She was right. What harm could she cause him? Despite her curves, she was slim, with little muscle, and it wasn't as if she could conceal a weapon anywhere, unless...

He looked at the dark triangle between her legs, and stifled a chuckle.

No, this woman posed absolutely no threat. And while he *would* kill her, as per his orders, there was no harm in coming closer and fulfilling a pretty lady's last request.

He walked fully into the candlelight. Her soft features were even more ravishing up close.

She offered him the sponge. "Take it."

He did, and she leaned her head back and lifted her hair.

"Be gentle with me," she whispered.

Lawson laid his rifle on the floor, ensuring it was out of the woman's reach. He may have been horny, but he wasn't an idiot.

"Wash me," she said.

He dipped the sponge into the bucket, wrung it out, and wiped her shoulders. She looked pretty clean to him, but who was he to argue? Squeezing the sponge over her breasts, he watched, fascinated, as the water dribbled towards her nipples. Could he touch them? Would let him?

"You're beautiful," she said, and Lawson almost burst out laughing. Even before the machete attack, he hadn't been beautiful. In fact, according to his mother, he had dropped out of the womb ugly as sin and twice as mean. His schoolmates gave him the nickname Pigface, and his first — and to date, only — girlfriend said she only dated him after a friend told her ugly guys were the best lays, because they would do anything out of gratitude.

Lawson had gotten pretty used to people telling him he was ugly, but when this woman — this goddess — told him with such unflinching sincerity that he was beautiful, he believed her.

A face like that could tell no lies.

The sponge fell from his hand. "Say that again," he said, and for the first time in decades, Lawson started to cry. The woman embraced him, bringing his head to her shoulder and letting him weep against her collarbone.

"That's right," she said. "Let it out. Let it all out."

Ashamed of his emotions, he sobbed while she stroked his hair and whispered exotic nothings into his ear. Like a trilling lullaby sung from a mother to a mewling infant, the nonsense words calmed him. They seeped into his flesh and wormed their way inside his brain, and when the woman raised his head and pressed her lips to his, he felt nothing but numbness, and the complete absence of hatred and fear and self-loathing. She pushed something into his eager mouth with her tongue, and he accepted it, swallowing the sticky lump gratefully.

"I love you," he said, and she smiled knowingly and stepped backwards into obsidian shadows that swallowed her whole. With tears streaming down his cheeks, Lawson waved goodbye. "I'll always love you."

He stood, staring at the darkness, then turned and headed back along the corridor to the walkway. There, with the lovely words of the woman ringing sweetly in his ears, he clambered onto the rails and balanced precariously atop them. The wind urged him onwards, and when he looked down at the warehouse floor — so cold, so hard — he smiled to himself.

"As you wish, my love," he said, then closed his eyes and let go of his conscious self, his body toppling forwards and hurtling through the air. He didn't know why, and he didn't need to, for when his head struck the floor and shattered in a welter of blood and bone and brain, all that mattered was that the woman — that perfect, beautiful woman — had told him to do it, and Travis Lawson was a man who followed orders.

It was what he did best.

27

BACK IN THE PENTHOUSE SUITE, RON GLANCED NERVOUSLY AT his phone for the hundredth time, and found no word from Duke amongst the missed calls and unread emails displayed on the lock screen.

Vivienne sat next to Nick on the sofa, the pair killing time by watching a rerun of an E! Entertainment special on their upcoming wedding. Over supposedly candid footage of the happy couple getting matching pedicures, the presenter waxed rhapsodic about the 'social event of the season' and reeled off a list of the expected guests.

"Stupid bitch didn't mention Glen Powell," muttered Vivienne. She chewed on a nail, and Ron leaned over and slapped her hand.

"You want ragged nails for your wedding?"

"I want to know if I'm *having* a wedding," she said, folding her arms and shuffling closer to Nick.

"Duke never lets me down," said Ron. "He'll take care of her."

"What, like he did last time?"

Ron cleared his throat. "This is different. He won't make the same mistake twice."

"I don't understand why you two are so worried," said Nick, his gaze never leaving the TV screen. "Who's Duke away to talk to?"

"I told you," said Vivienne. "The catering company is threatening to pull out, and Duke's going to straighten things out with them. But if he fails..."

"Then we hire another catering company." Nick placed a comforting hand on her inner thigh, much to Ron's disgust. "It's not the end of the world."

It was Ron who had come up with the lie about the catering company. How else could they explain the situation to Nick? *Oh, by the way, the daughter of the wizard who cast a love spell on you wants to kill us all now. If we don't snuff her first, you might wake up and remember that you don't actually love Vivienne. Happy wedding day!*

Keeping him in the dark was easier, and, luckily, since the spell, the man was too vacuous to question anything.

"Hey look, there's us!" he said, pointing at the screen and grinning. The shot was of Nick and Vivienne at their engagement party, dancing in the middle of the room and pausing to share a passionate kiss for the camera. In the background, Ron was chatting to Sydney Sweeney, his arm around the actress's shoulders as she visibly strained to get away from him. "And there's you, Ron!"

"Fuck off," he snarled, keen to forget his failed attempts to woo the beautiful starlet.

"Sorry, dad."

"And don't call me dad."

Ron glanced at his phone. Ring, dammit! Duke had been gone for two hours already, and hadn't checked in once. It was concerning. He saw Vivienne look at him, and he smiled.

"He'll call any minute now," he said. She was biting her nails again. "Just wait and see."

There were toads *everywhere.*

Deep in the bowels of the ruined warehouse, Singh waded through a swarm of the amphibious bastards, wondering where the fuck they were coming from. They hopped down the basement corridor, their translucent bodies whacking against his ankles. He stooped and lifted one by the leg, inspecting it under the glare of his flashlight.

The little freak had no eyes.

He tossed it over his shoulder and carried on, shining his flashlight across the walls and over the unceasing wave of sightless beasts.

There.

His beam settled on a hole in the floor, from which the toads fled in droves. Singh advanced, aiming his flashlight into the murky opening. There was a short drop, and then the ground angled down and out of sight. Did it lead to the sewers? Could the woman possibly be hiding out there?

Only one way to find out.

He lowered himself into the hole. When his feet touched solid rock, he pressed the button on his earpiece.

"Alpha Two here. Found an underground passageway in the west basement corridor. I'm going in."

His earpiece crackled. *"Roger that,"* whispered Duke. *"Check-in back at the entrance in ten minutes. All clear so far."*

There was no word from Lawson, but that was as expected. Lawson only spoke when spoken to. Singh sometimes wondered why Duke kept him around. When *he* was in charge, Lawson would be the first to go.

He hoped that day would come soon. While he respected Duke, the man was not getting any younger, and Singh had his eyes set firmly on the prize; the chief of security role. He was fed up with his Alpha Two callsign.

He wanted to be Alpha *One*.

It was only fair. He was stronger and hungrier, and had they been two lions, Singh would have challenged his elder to a battle for leadership over the pack. Sadly, they were men, and there was a code of honor they had to follow. But one day...

Singh crouched to navigate the tunnel. The roof scraped his back, the frenzied toads smacking wetly against him. Twenty feet in, the tunnel curved to the left, the sharp ceiling getting lower with each step. He moved onto his hands and knees, but as the roof continued sloping, he soon found he had to lie on his chest and drag himself along with his elbows to make any progress.

He paused, deciding whether to proceed. His shoulders scraped the walls of the narrow tunnel, barely leaving enough room for the fleeing toads to pass by. If he kept going, he'd risk getting stuck. Sweat dripped down his neck, and a brief moment of claustrophobic terror rippled through him, not helped by the blind amphibians that whacked relentlessly against his face.

"Fuck off," he grunted, and as he spoke, a toad leaped towards his mouth like the fucker was aiming for it. The slimy body touched his lips, and Singh clamped them shut.

That was the last straw.

He shuffled backwards. If crawling through the tunnel had been slow-going, trying to reverse using only his elbows was even more demanding. But Singh was a patient man, and if he had to take the journey one inch at a time, then he damn well—

Wait...

Shit.

Fuck.

Shit.

Something was stopping him. He looked back, unable to see beyond the low rocks that jabbed into his spine and shoulders. Instead, he attempted to move forwards to free himself. It was no use.

He was stuck.

Stay calm.

Hysteria was his greatest enemy now. He had gotten into this situation, and it would take a level head to extricate himself. Drawing in a deep breath, he exhaled and tried again.

"Fuck!"

It didn't help that the toads kept coming, building up in front of his face and smothering him. They obscured his flashlight beam, and he tried to shove them away. What the fuck was preventing him from moving? His legs were free — he could kick them — and he felt little pressure on his body from the rocks.

His vest? Was his tactical vest snagged?

It was worth a shot.

The vest had a built-in quick-release lever for speedy removal. The armor was held together by a thick cord that threaded through the various parts, and one sharp pull of the metal bar around his neck would yank the cord out of the vest. There were too many fasteners to fully dismantle it, but removing the cord should loosen the armor enough for him to slip free.

Presuming, of course, he could reach it.

He bent his arm back through the swathe of toads, groping for the lever. With difficulty, he tore the Velcro around the neck open and stretched for the small metal bar.

Duke's voice hissed through the earpiece. *"Alpha One in position."*

Singh was too focused on freeing himself to reply. His fingers found the lever, and he pulled.

Nothing happened.

"Fuck," he snarled. *"Fuck!"*

He should never have bellowed that second fuck, because the moment he did, the toads took their chance.

One hopped into his mouth.

Singh gagged as the slippery creature landed on his tongue and burrowed down his throat. Lying awkwardly, with one arm straight ahead and the other contorted into position at his neckline, he tried to retrieve the toad, craning his neck to allow his hand access.

Too late.

The foul beast had wedged in his windpipe. Only now did Singh truly start to panic. He was choking, and he was trapped, and no one could help him. He yanked hard on the tactical vest quick-release, and this time it came free. The vest slackened. It was only an inch, but it was enough. He pushed back, squashing toads beneath his hands, and freed himself from the vest.

The toad seemed to have liquified in his throat, leaving a spicy taste that trickled down his esophagus. He spat it out, but the burning sensation remained.

Dragging his rifle and flashlight, he eventually made it far enough to spin and pivot into facing the right direction. From there, he crawled until he came to the tunnel opening and scrambled free. God, his stomach felt like it was on fire.

His throat, too. As he blundered along the corridor, he wondered if the toad was venomous.

"Is anyone there?" Duke asked over the radio. *"Anybody?"*

Singh detected a rare note of panic in Duke's voice. He put his finger to the earpiece and pressed, but when he opened his mouth, no sounds come out.

Just smoke.

He clutched his abdomen. Through his shirt, his skin prickled from the heat. It reminded him of being a child in England, when his mum would give him a hot water bottle to cuddle when he was poorly. Except this time, it felt like the boiling water had been poured directly down his throat and into his stomach.

"Huuuugghhh," he gasped, as he staggered towards the exit. This wasn't good.

This wasn't good *at all.*

28

WHERE THE FUCK WERE THEY?

Duke waited by the van, nervously spinning one of his pistols. Neither of his men had made it out yet, and now they weren't responding over the radio. Sirens wailed in the distance, and he tucked his gun back in its holster. Dammit, they should have stuck together. But it's not like they were three bubble-headed co-eds in some crappy horror movie. They were heavily armed and ex-military. This mission should have been a walk in the fuckin' park.

So what if the woman used magic? Her father had taken almost half-an-hour to cast his love spell, and her powers couldn't possibly compare to his. For a start, she was considerably younger and less experienced than him, and that wasn't counting the fact she was a woman, which meant she would lack the killer instinct required for this line of work.

He tried his radio again. "Alpha One in position. Can anyone hear me?"

Fuck's sake!

He thought he heard something in the van, but before

he could check, movement from the warehouse caught his eye.

Singh!

All that worry for nothing. Duke allowed himself a chuckle and waved the man over.

In response, Singh shrieked.

In all their years working together, Duke had never once heard Singh scream. The mercenary was cold and merciless, and although he would occasionally laugh at a dirty joke or in the face of a torture victim, Duke hadn't been sure Singh was capable of normal human emotion until that bone-chilling shriek.

Slowly, he crossed the road. Singh had fallen to his knees, and he appeared to be... glowing? His neck and face flared yellow, and plumes of black smoke billowed from between his lips.

Duke hesitated. "What's she done to you, man?"

"Hhhhuuuurtsss," Singh wheezed. His quivering hands took the hem of his sweater and lifted it.

"Shit," said Duke.

Singh's stomach was on fire...

Inside him.

The blaze raged beneath the walls of his skin, the flames illuminating Singh's ribs and intestines like a macabre shadow play. It stretched to his gullet, showcasing the veins that threaded throughout him, and when Singh opened his mouth, Duke saw the flickering light behind his teeth. Instead of another scream, a ball of wild flame erupted. Singh's lips withered from the blast, his eyes twinkling like lights on a Christmas tree. The bloodshot orbs puckered, then popped, dribbling down his cheeks like ejaculate, as more flames sparked and burned in his vacant eye sockets.

His sizzling skin blackened and cracked until it could contain the inferno no longer.

Duke saw it coming. He shielded his eyes and backed away as his colleague burst into cataclysmic flame. The miniature explosion lit up the street, and then, as quickly as the pyrotechnic marvel had appeared, it was gone.

Singh's charred bones dropped to the sidewalk with a coarse rattle.

Duke placed a finger to his ear and pressed the button. "Are you there, Lawson?" Their codenames no longer mattered. "Singh's dead."

A new voice came over the in-ear speaker. An unexpected one.

"Did you bring my invitation?"

"Jesus," said Duke.

"I hope you did. I've already picked out a dress."

"Where's Lawson, you bitch? What have you done with him?"

The woman laughed. Duke tore the earpiece out and hurled it into the gutter, then turned and ran towards the van. He'd have to come back, of course. He couldn't return to Ron without the witch's severed head, not if he valued his own life. But this time, he'd be prepared. He'd make some calls, get a full squad together with all the firepower they could muster, and blow the entire place sky fucking high.

First, though, he had to get out of here. He threw open the van door, his heart pounding dangerously out of control, and—

"Oh, you gotta be fucking kidding me," he said, as his gaze fell upon the enormous, pale yellow python coiled on and around the driver's seat. It stared at him with sleepy eyes, its tongue darting from the broad, smirking mouth. Duke reached for his pistol, not realizing how quickly a snake of that size could move. It lunged from the van, knocking him flat and weaving its wide body around him.

He tried to struggle free, but the serpent only wrapped itself tighter, constricting both his movements and his breathing. His arms were pressed to his sides, his fingertips scratching at the useless firearms on his hips. The serpent's face rested next to his, the scales sparkling in the moonlight. It could crush him if it wanted to.

Instead, it waited.

Duke heard the scuff of approaching footsteps. With a Burmese python compressing him, he tilted his head back and saw the sorcerer's daughter strolling casually towards him with a warm smile on her lips. She kneeled beside him.

"Mr. Duke," she said, stroking her hand down the serpent's spine. "How nice to see you again. The last time we met, you were sitting in my father's favorite chair and watching your men rape me."

"They weren't my men," he gasped, the snake tensing around him. "I... I didn't approve of what they did to you."

"You didn't stop them though, did you?"

Duke had no answer to that.

She ran her fingers over his face. "And now, I believe, you have something I require."

"I don't have your fucking invitation."

"Mr. Duke, please..." She traced a line around his eye socket. "It's not the invitation I want."

Pinching his lashes, Anong lifted his eyelid, higher and higher, then slipped her fingers under the delicate flap of skin. Her nail scratched the inside of the lid as she forced her digits further in, scraping at the meat around his eyeball. Duke yelled in agony as she hooked her fingers and inserted them all the way into the socket. She curled them around the mushy organ and pulled.

"Stop!" Duke begged. "Please, stop! I didn't do anything!"

"And that, Mr. Duke," she said, tugging harder, "is the problem."

Duke's sight blurred. He heard the optic nerve tear as the eyeball detached, and half his vision went utterly, hopelessly dark. Duke wept from one eye as blood spurted across his face. Was this how his life was to end? Wrapped in a snake and ritually slaughtered for the sake of Ron Jarvis's daughter getting some — as she herself had described it — hot dick action?

The indignity of it all... the fucking indignity!

Anong reached into her dress and removed a small leather bag. She carefully untied the cord that bound it.

"And now," she said, reaching inside the bag, "I have something for *you,* Mr. Duke." She placed her fingers above and below his empty socket.

"Open wide."

29

It was two in the morning, and still no word from Duke. Ron rose from his chair and looked restlessly out the window. The streets far below thrummed with traffic. Dammit, Duke should have called by now.

Nick, unaware of the high stakes at play, had retired to bed on Ron's insistence, while Vivienne had spent the last ten minutes throwing up in the bathroom. He heard the door unlock, and she shambled into place on the couch.

"Nerves?" he asked her. She shrugged. "Could be worse. You'll be thinner for the wedding."

She ignored the remark. "Did Stan—"

"No." He left the window and took his seat again, lighting a cigar. "Go to bed, pumpkin. I'll wake you if I hear anything."

"I couldn't sleep. Not tonight." She lifted her shirt and checked her stomach. The words were still etched into her skin.

Ron winced. This was all his fault. He should never have taken her to that damn shaman. And, he supposed, he probably shouldn't have killed the old man. But how much trouble could Suwin's daughter really be? She had made plain her views on the use of magic.

God, kids could be such assholes.

He looked at his own offspring, in her fluffy robe and slippers, and wondered if his life would have been easier without her. Of course it would have. And any parent who said otherwise was a fucking liar.

The phone rang. Vivienne shrieked in surprise, and even Ron's stomach jumped. The ringing was coming from the landline, which was connected only to the downstairs lobby. He snatched up the receiver. "Talk to me."

"Sir, uhhh... Stan Duke is on his way up to see you. I tried to stop him, but—"

"Why the hell would you stop him?" Ron barked. "I've been waiting all goddam night for him! What's your name? Because you're fired."

"It's Deacon, sir. I tried to stop him because, well... something's wrong."

"Wrong? What do you mean?"

"Is it him, daddy?" asked Vivienne.

"Wait a second, your father's talking."

"Excuse me, sir?" said Deacon.

"Not you, dipshit. What were you saying about—"

The elevator dinged its arrival.

"Never mind. He's here."

"Am I still fired, sir?"

"Absolutely," said Ron, and he slammed the phone down.

The elevator doors slid open.

"Where the hell have you been, Duke?" bellowed Ron as he strode towards the elevator, Vivienne following close behind. A mixture of relief and anger washed over him. "We've been... *oh.*"

He froze before the open doors, staring at the man inside, who certainly *looked* like Stan Duke. He had the same face and hair, and the same build, although this man... well, there was no nice way of putting it.

Stan Duke looked like a walking corpse.

Dried blood coated his face, and his clothes were filthy and torn, revealing purple welts and ugly bruising. One eye was sunken, the other caked in gore.

"Duke, you look like shit," said Ron, displaying his usual tact. "What the fuck happened?"

The elevator doors started to shut, and Ron used his foot to halt them. Duke remained in place, and Ron noticed he was carrying a small parcel, gift-wrapped in gold paper and tied with a pink satin bow. There was a card attached.

"You coming in or what?" He ushered Duke into the apartment. Clutching his box, the man waddled out of the elevator on stiff legs, his ripped trousers stained red with blood. Ron and Vivienne shared a glance.

"Well? You gonna tell us what happened?"

"Is she *dead?*" snarled Vivienne.

Duke laid the package on the glass table and sat heavily. His head flopped back, and he wheezed something inaudible.

"What was that?" asked Ron. "What did you say?"

"Open it," breathed Duke. His lips didn't move, the words rising ghost-like from between them. He slid the package across the table with a limp hand. The lower portion was damp, and it left a faint red residue on the glass. *"Open the box."*

Vivienne reached for it, and Ron stopped her.

"Wait," he said. "That's blood."

Vivienne clapped her hands together excitedly. "Blood? Is it her head, like I asked?" She removed the card and set it aside, then smiled at Duke. "Stanny, I could kiss you!" A trickle of blood-flecked drool rolled down his chin. "Maybe not right now, though," she added, and reached for the package.

"The bitch is *de-ead*," she sang, "and I've got her *he-ead*." She untied the satin ribbon and dug her nails into the wrapping paper, tearing it apart to reveal a cardboard box pockmarked with bloodstains.

"Fucking bitch tried to ruin *my* wedding," said Vivienne. She opened the box. "Well, let's see who has the last—"

She screamed.

The box fell from her hands, striking the edge of the table. It hit the floor, bounced, and released its foul contents.

Ron stood immobile, gazing down between his feet. They looked like... they weren't... they couldn't be... why would—

"It's dicks," said Vivienne. She gagged. "It's a pair of fucking *dicks*."

She wasn't wrong.

Two severed penises lay on the wooden floor like revolting, ugly worms.

...worms...

They hadn't been neatly sliced off, either. The torn sex organs appeared to have lost a tug-of-war with a pitbull.

"Oh god," said Vivienne, throwing a hand to her mouth and running from the room.

Ron turned to Duke. "What the fuck is this?" he asked. "Why did you bring me a box of dicks?" Unsure what to do — he couldn't exactly call Perlah to clean the mess up — he picked up the box with hands that trembled with rage.

Something plopped out and splatted between his feet.

Wearily, Ron looked down. Duke had told him he was

bringing two men to deal with the shaman's daughter, and it didn't take a genius to figure out where this third dick had come from. Through the glass table, he saw Duke's blood-soaked crotch, and he, too, felt bile rise.

Duke started to laugh. It came out as a desiccated chuckle.

"You're dead, aren't you?" Ron asked quietly, afraid of the response. He gazed at the man's eyes, one his usual blue, the other — which, on closer inspection, looked to have been crudely inserted into the socket — a light brown.

He leaned both hands on the table. "Are you watching me? Are you looking through that eye?"

Duke laughed harder, and Ron pounded his fist off the glass.

"You bitch... I'll fucking kill you myself." He stormed out of the room and into the kitchen, returning moments later with the largest knife he could find. Looming over Duke, his faithful chief of security for over twenty years, he readied the blade.

Duke's jaw dropped open, a thin snake unfurling from within and slithering onto the table.

"Oh, you motherfucker," growled Ron. "I'm gonna fucking *kill* you."

He stabbed the knife violently, and when Vivienne, her stomach empty from throwing up twice in ten minutes, entered the room and walked in on her father burrowing an eight-inch kitchen knife into Stan Duke's eyeball, and saw the snake coiled on the floor next to three severed dicks, she simply turned on her heels and headed back to the toilet bowl.

It was going to be a long night.

30

"Jesus wept," said Ron, as he wiped his bloody hands on his suit jacket and surveyed the carnage.

Duke sat slumped in the chair, blood flowing from his eye socket. On the table was the package, which now contained a flattened snake and a stained kitchen knife in addition to the three severed dicks. It looked like a serial killer's garage sale.

"Jesus fucking *wept.*"

He would need someone to destroy the evidence. Normally he would have called Duke, but his former security chief also needed to be disposed of. It was a sad end to a good man.

As he considered who to call, he spotted the note that had come attached to the package. It was addressed to Vivienne, and in her absence, he opened it.

Looking forward to the wedding.
X

He scrunched the paper and tossed it in the garbage. Vivienne was still dry-heaving in the bathroom, so he washed his hands and decided to call Marty Hooper.

Marty was Ron's number one guy at Jarvis Media, an unscrupulous, cut-throat businessman who reminded Ron of himself. Hooper answered on the second ring. *"What's up, Ron?"*

"Marty, I need a cleanup crew at the penthouse. *Very* discrete. Think you can handle it?"

"Of course, Ron. I'll deal with it personally."

"Good man. I'll be waiting."

He hung up, pleased that Hooper had refrained from asking for details. The kid would go far in business. Ron had secretly hoped Hooper and Vivienne would hit it off — he would be a much more capable son-in-law than that dead-beat Pulaski — but Vivienne wasn't interested. She always did have a thing for those hippy Hollywood types.

Her dainty footsteps approached, and Ron quickly grabbed a blanket from the sofa and covered the corpse with it. She hovered in the doorway, her face pale and shaken. "What are we going to do, daddy?"

He sighed. "There's a cleanup crew on the way. They'll take Duke and the box down to—"

"I'm not talking about that," she snapped. "I'm talking about my fucking wedding."

"Of course. How foolish of me to think you gave a shit about anyone else." She looked shocked, but his patience had worn thin. "Go wake Nick. I need his help."

"I... I can't," she said. "I give him sleeping pills every night to stop him trying to fu—"

"Fine," he interrupted. He felt nauseous enough without having to hear about his daughter's sex life. "Guess you're gonna have to help me. The cleanup crew will be here soon, but Duke's gonna start to smell, and once you get corpse stink in a building, it's impossible to get rid of." He ran a hand through his hair and thought of Barry Benchley and the worms. "Believe me, I know."

∽

Marty Hooper's crew arrived a little after three, by which point Ron had managed to manhandle Duke's body onto a spare bed sheet. Vivienne helped by pouring herself a glass of whiskey and telling her father to be careful because he wasn't getting any younger.

Thankfully, Hooper's crew were less useless, and in a matter of minutes, the evidence was on en route to the basement furnace. After, the men returned and scrubbed the penthouse clean. Hooper tried making flirtatious small talk with Vivienne, so she woke Nick and made him help her light some scented candles. By the time the crew left, the room stank like a whorehouse, which everyone agreed was a distinct improvement.

Afterwards, the three of them sat drinking, the men smoking cigars.

Ron took a sip of scotch and set his glass on the armrest. "I think we oughta cancel the wedding." He didn't look at Vivienne, but he could imagine her expression. "Just for a little while, until we've got a handle on the situation."

"No fucking way," she said. "I'm not letting some witch spoil my first wedding."

"Your *only* wedding," said Nick.

Vivienne patted his knee. "That's right, baby." She looked at her father. "There has to be another option."

"Three of my best men are dead," said Ron. "What else do you want from me?"

"We don't know Duke's men are dead. They could still be—"

"Still be what? Wandering around LA with no dicks? You think they've gone for dinner and movie? They're *dead,* Vivienne. And if this wedding goes ahead, it might be you next. Or me." He poured the dregs of the scotch into his glass, and muttered, "Or all three of us."

"Shit," said Nick. "That's one hell of an aggressive catering company."

"For fuck's sake," snapped Vivienne. "We're not talking about a catering company! It's a witch! A fucking witch is trying to kill us!"

"A witch?" He didn't seem phased. "Why would she do that?"

Vivienne realized she'd said too much. She looked to Ron for help, and he obliged.

"She's in love with you, Nick. The witch wants to marry you, and she'll kill Vivienne to get to you."

"I won't let that happen." Nick shook his head resolutely. "I'm my own man, and I make my own decisions as to who I love."

"Yeah, sure..." said Ron, and Vivienne glared at him. "Anyway, she's been using magic to ruin your wedding, and we're trying to stop her. We didn't tell you because—"

"Because I didn't want to worry you," Vivienne interjected. "But now you know, any ideas on how to fight a witch?"

Nick looked thoughtful. "A witch, huh? Well, now you mention it, I was in a movie once where these sexy teenagers in bikinis got trapped in a—"

"Quiet," said Ron. "The adults are talking."

"What if you sent more men?" asked Vivienne. "Like, *hundreds* more. Don't you have contacts in the military?"

Nick sat forwards. "No, seriously, listen to me. It was a low-budget movie from when I was a stuntman. *Bikini Voodoo Kickboxers*, it was called, and in it, these hot bikini babes got stuck in a bayou swamp and pissed off a voodoo priest."

"What the fuck are you talking about?" asked Ron. There was no time for this. They needed a plan, not the synopsis of a B-movie.

"So," Nick continued, "this voodoo priest starts killing them one-by-one and taking their bikinis as trophies." He paused. "Tops *and* bottoms."

"Get to the fucking point."

"Yeah, okay. So the lead actress — you can tell she was gonna be the survivor, because she's the only one wearing a full bathing suit and not a bikini — anyway, she finds a *good* voodoo priest, and he helps her."

"Shut up and get the fuck out of my home," said Ron.

"No, wait," Vivienne interrupted. "I think he's onto something."

"I think he's on drugs." Ron rubbed his forehead. Then, to no one in particular, he said, "Of all the imbeciles in the world, she wants to marry this one."

"Daddy, listen to him! We're up against a witch—"

"The daughter of a shaman," he corrected.

"Whatever. What Nick's saying is, why don't we hire a *good* shaman to help us? Someone to fight her, like in *Bikini Voodoo Kickboxers.*"

"And where the hell do we find one of those?" said Ron, though the stupid suggestion had unlocked something in his mind, and it whirred with possibilities. He might not know where to locate a shaman... but he knew somebody who would.

He pulled out his phone.

"Who are you calling?" asked Vivienne.

Before he could reply, Edgar Charon answered, despite it being the middle of the night. From what he remembered of the man, Edgar only slept two hours a night.

"Good morning, Ron," he said in a bored voice. *"Trouble sleeping?"*

"Edgar? I need your help again."

"Yeah, I imagine you're in a whole world of shit right now. I heard what you did, and let me be the first to say, you made a huge mistake."

"Word gets around fast, huh?"

"It does in the circles I travel in. So why are you calling?"

Ron looked at Vivienne. This was it, his chance to make it right. For good, this time.

"I, uh, need more shamen."

"Shamans," said Edgar.

"What?"

"The plural of shaman is shamans, not shamen."

It all sounded the same to Ron over the phone. "Okay, whatever. I need more shamans. As many as you can round up." He chuckled. "Guess that's a sentence you don't hear every day."

"You'd be surprised."

"I suppose I would." Ron didn't know what went on at the famously secretive Rylak Corporation where Edgar worked, but he knew they were involved in some dark shit. "So what do you say?"

"Ron, do you realize what you're asking me?"

"I do. You know I'm good for the payment."

"It's not that. You understand how difficult it is to get a bunch of shamans in the same room? Those guys are volatile."

"I only need four or five."

"Four or five? Jesus, Ron. What d'you think, that everyone in

Thailand practices black magic? You ass. There are less than ten of these guys across the whole country, especially since you fucking killed one of them."

Ron gripped his phone with sweaty hands. "I know, Edgar. And... I'm sorry." He winced at the word. "But can you do it?"

A long silence followed. Ron checked the screen to ensure they were still connected.

"It's not going to be easy," said Edgar.

Ron smiled. "That's why I called you."

"Yeah, but convincing them will be difficult when they know who they're up against. Ron, you crazy bastard, you started a war with the most powerful shaman in Thailand."

"Bullshit," he snapped. "We killed him. I don't care how powerful that bastard was... we fucking *killed* him."

Down the phone, Edgar laughed. His laughter was shrill and cruel, the way Ron remembered it. *"Oh, Ron, you sweet fool. You didn't kill the most powerful shaman in Thailand."*

He paused, letting his words sink in.

"You killed her father."

PART III

THE WEDDING

31

"YOU LOOK BEAUTIFUL."

Ron Jarvis adjusted his daughter's veil and stepped back to admire her.

Vivienne, an extravagant vision in handmade lace, ran her hands down a dress that had cost an eye-watering two million, and said, "I know." The V-neck bodice flowed into a demure floor-length skirt festooned with hundreds of thousands of tiny sparkling crystals that shimmered under the lights.

Two million bucks, thought Ron. *And worth every cent.*

The big day had arrived — the matrimonial union of Vivienne Jarvis and Nick Alexander Pulaski — and no one present knew quite what to expect, especially after one fraught month of uncertainty, during which none of the family had left the penthouse for fear that *she* would be there.

The most powerful shaman in Thailand, according to Edgar Charon.

Yet nobody had seen Anong since her attack on Vivienne in the bathtub. Well, no one who was still alive. It was as if she had fallen off the face of the Earth, and although the scars she had left on Vivienne were now a distant memory, thanks to some highly experimental — and very expensive — surgery, her fearful presence seemed to linger, even if her corporeal form was absent.

"Hey, they're playing your song," said Ron, as the faint strains of Ed Sheeran seeped through the doors, signaling the beginning of the ceremony. He held out his arm. "Shall we?"

She looked nervously up at him. "Do you think—"

"Everything is going to be fine. I promise."

"Okay," she said, and hooked her arm around his. "Thank you, daddy."

He squeezed her lovingly. "Anything for my special pumpkin."

Vivienne took a breath. "I guess it's now or never," she said, and together they walked to the door, stepping in perfect synchronicity like they had practiced. Ron pushed the doors open, revealing the rarely used chapel on the thirty-ninth floor of Jarvis Tower.

A red carpet had been rolled out towards the low stage, upon which stood Nick, wearing a custom tuxedo specifically tailored to flatter his muscular physique, and the priest. On either side of the men were burly security guards with concealed weapons and earpieces, while Marty Hooper, recently promoted to chief of security, skulked by the door. There were no photographers, no bridesmaids, no celebrity guests... in fact, other than the security guards, there were no guests at all. It was a private ceremony, one week ahead of schedule, and the whole affair felt more akin to a dress rehearsal.

It was exactly as Ron had planned.

He nodded at Hooper, who acknowledged him and spoke quietly into a radio.

Everything was set.

They arrived at the stage, and Ed Sheeran faded out over the speakers. Ron helped Vivienne climb the three stairs before handing her off to her fiancé. She took her place, looking resplendent in virginal white, and he retreated to his seat to watch the service unfold.

The priest — one of Hooper's team, a firearm tucked under his cassock — grinned crookedly at the happy couple, and addressed the room.

"Gentlemen," he said in a thick Bronx accent, "we are gathered here today to celebrate the, uhh..." — he glanced at the crumpled paper in his hand — "holy union of this here coupe." He peered at the words. "Wait, I mean couple."

Ron bit back a snort of derision at the man's incompetence. It was a more familiar emotion than the nervousness that fluttered in his stomach, and he welcomed it.

The security guard-turned-priest cleared his throat. Then he looked away, hawked up a wad of phlegm, and spat on the carpet. "Uh, like I was sayin', it's, uh..." He checked his paper again. "Oh yeah, I almost forgot. Before we start, if anyone has any, y'know, objections, then speak now or forever hold your, uh, peace."

This was it.

The big moment.

Ron held his breath and looked at the door. The room was motionless, apart from anticipatory hands twitching over guns and the collective thudding of hearts.

Would she come?

If so, where *was* she?

Where was the sorceress?

"Hey, you want me to carry on?" asked the priest.

"Wait a minute," Ron whispered without looking at him, his gaze never leaving the door. Any moment now, she would appear in all her evil splendor. He was sure of it. They just had to wait.

They just had to be patient.

Seconds ticked by.

Ron checked his watch.

"Daddy?" said Vivienne. "I don't think she's—"

The door opened.

Ron couldn't help smiling at the woman's impeccable sense of timing. Hell, in a way, he respected her. The chick had bigger balls than most men.

Anong entered the chapel dressed in a figure-hugging Thai bridal dress, carrying a bouquet of flowers in one hand and swinging a severed head in the other. Ron recognized the head as that of the security guard positioned outside the chapel doors.

She sure knew how to make an entrance.

"First I don't receive an invitation," Anong announced. "And now I find you're starting without me. Where is this American hospitality I've heard about?"

"We didn't think you were coming," said Ron with a sudden surge of confidence. The entire rest of his life hinged on the next few minutes, and the idea thrilled him. "But now you're here, why don't you take a seat and enjoy the show?"

Standing in the doorway, Anong released the severed head. It thumped dully to the floor. "No, thank you. I won't be staying. I just came to collect what's mine."

"And what's that?" asked Ron. "My deal was with your father."

"And when you killed him," Anong said icily, "the deal passed on to *me*." She looked around the room and scoffed.

"Did you really think moving the date forwards one week would stop me? That I wouldn't *know?*"

"We thought it was worth a try," said Ron. He looked up at his daughter. "Didn't we, pumpkin?"

"Yeah," said Vivienne. He could tell she was afraid.

She needn't be.

His plan was in motion.

Anong offered her hand to Vivienne from across the room. "Come with me. *Now.*"

Vivienne looked uncertain. Then, her resolve seemed to strengthen. "Why don't you come and get me... you *cunt?*"

Anong laughed. She glanced at the security guards. "Honestly, Mr. Jarvis. I expected more from you. Those last men you sent me... I thought you might have learned your lesson. Instead, like a typical rich American businessman, you thought that more guns... *bigger* guns... would somehow be enough to protect you. Your small-mindedness never ceases to disappoint me."

"You're absolutely right," said Ron. "I guess you'd better take what's rightfully yours. My daughter on her wedding day."

"I think," Anong said, "that I'll do just..."

She walked forwards, leaving the safety of the doorway and crossing the threshold.

"...that."

The door slammed shut behind her.

"Now!" shouted Ron, and on his command, huge yellow banners unfurled from the ceiling, covering every square inch of wall. Upon the banners were thousands of words in a language he couldn't hope to understand, each symbol painstakingly daubed by hand in — so he had been told — alligator blood.

"No!" shrieked Anong. She staggered against the door,

and when her spine touched the banner, it burned. Smoke rose from her back, and she yelled in pain and anger. Four robed men stepped forwards from behind the stage. One held a small drum, upon which he tapped an arrhythmic beat, while all four chanted in unison.

Anong shrank back from the powerful psychic onslaught, her fingers twisting into talons.

"Well, well, well," Ron said, striding towards her. "Looks like ol' Ron Jarvis was one step ahead of the sorceress this time! Bet you didn't think I'd fight fire with fire, huh?"

"Like in *Bikini Voodoo Kickboxers!*" shouted Nick.

"Shut up!" Ron roared. Fuck! That asshole had ruined his big speech. He turned back to Anong. She fought against the magic that bound her, managing to take a step closer. "I thought you said you could hold her?" Ron called uneasily.

The gathered shamans chanted louder, the pounding of the drum increasing in volume and tempo. Anong reached for him, her body vibrating like a tuning fork, her face contorted into a frozen cry of fury. Vein-like attenuations burned within her, radiating an unnatural, glimmering incandescence. Smoke rose, her flesh bubbling, then spurting.

Good god, thought Ron.

She was *melting.*

Taking a chance, he stepped closer and grabbed a handful of her dress. After all the trouble she had caused him, he didn't just want to kill her. He wanted to humiliate her. "Let's see you for what you really are," he said, and tore the clothing from her body.

The chanting men closed in.

Ron watched in delighted fascination as Anong's skin dissolved. The tips of her fingers hung in globules of fleshy ooze, her breasts collapsing and dripping down her beautiful, naked body, a body he had desired since first laying eyes on it. He knew he could never have it, so to see her like this, stripped of her clothes and her power and, yes, her *flesh,* was simultaneously the most repulsive and erotic display he'd ever witnessed.

The melted tissue pooled around her feet, her face peeling away to expose the nightmare visage beneath; a scorched, shrieking skull. The chanting reached a deafening volume, as the last of Anong's disguise slipped away, leaving a ghoulish skeleton coated in charred muscle.

"Not so sexy now, are you?" Ron shouted. To him, it was the most profoundly degrading insult to *any* woman.

Anong's eyes blazed with fire. Her whole body did. But Ron was convinced of one thing; the bitch was going nowhere.

He glanced at Vivienne. "Come on, pumpkin. Get down here and let's finish this."

Hitching her dress up, Vivienne hopped down from the stage and marched to her father's side.

"You didn't honestly think *this* was my wedding, did you?" She struck Anong's skeletal cheek with an open hand. Black flakes crumbled from the witch's face and fluttered to the red carpet. "No press? No catering? No *Glen Powell?* How dumb are you?"

Anong's rigid arms cracked and splintered as she tried to reach for her.

"Yeah, nice try, bitch," said Vivienne. "But now it's *my* turn."

She lifted her dress, removing a switchblade from her garter belt. At the press of a button, the wickedly sharp blade flicked out before Anong's eyes. "How about some revenge for what you did to me in the bathtub?"

Turning the knife in her hand, she stuck the blade into

Anong, piercing her blackened abdomen. The witch screamed as Vivienne etched slow, deep cuts into her crispy flesh like she was carving a well-done steak.

Ron smiled in approval as his little girl stabbed and hacked at the woman. Blood that looked like glowing amber sap flowed down Anong's stomach and legs, but through the bubbling liquid, the letters were plain to see.

FUCK YOU

Vivienne cut the last stroke of the second U, and gazed at her handiwork. "How does it feel?" She slapped the woman again, hard enough to dislodge a slab of meat from her cheek and expose the white bone beneath. *"How does it fucking feel?"*

Anong's face twisted into a malevolent grimace. She turned her hand, drawing the fingers into a fist, and muttered to herself.

"Wait, what's she doing?" asked Ron.

Too late.

A high-pitched whine exploded in his head like a thousand needles jabbing into his eardrums. He clapped his hands over his ears, but nothing could shut the dreadful sound out. It wasn't just affecting him, either; Vivienne had fallen to her knees, blood pouring from her nostrils, while Nick was doubled over and vomiting. The four shamans, sent from Thailand by Edgar Charon for the princely sum of one million dollars apiece, continued their chanted invocations, but they, too, were in agony. Blood gushed from their noses, their ears, their eyes.

The drummed rhythm faltered, allowing Anong to take a corpse-like step closer.

She was too powerful.

"Hooper!" Ron cried, hoping his security chief could hear him, but when he looked in the direction of Stan Duke's replacement, the man was screaming in hellish torment.

Fuck it, thought Ron.

The time for games was over.

He staggered towards Hooper, the dreadful noise rising to an eardrum-shattering crescendo, and reached for the man's leg, where a twenty-four-inch machete was strapped. Ron drew the blade from its sheath and turned to the sorceress.

He lumbered closer as she slowly looked in his direction.

One of the shamans ejected a mouthful of blood and collapsed, clutching his heart.

Time was almost up.

"Fuck you!" Ron roared, as he brought the machete down on the sorceress's forearm with all his remaining might. The blade cut deep, burying into the bone. Anong yelled, closing her eyes, and at once, the spell was broken. The whine dissipated, replaced by the quiet moans and sobs of the security guards, and the frenzied chanting of the shamans.

Ron wasted no time. He raised the gleaming blade again, and brought it down on the same spot. Fuelled by anger and hatred and pure adrenaline, the machete cut through Anong's arm. The limb hit the floor, landing on the plush red carpet like the broken branch of a dead and ancient tree.

The fingers on her other hand began to curl.

"I don't fucking think so," he said, and hacked at Anong's hand, chopping her fingers cleanly off. He attacked her shoulder, the machete whacking viciously into her flesh, exposing muscle and cracked white bone. It took five blows

— her shoulder blade kept getting in the way — but when her right arm joined the other on the floor, Ron allowed himself a triumphant holler.

Vivienne, her expensive dress drenched in her own blood, ran to her father and hugged him.

"I love you, daddy," she said.

"I love you too, pumpkin."

As father-daughter bonding moments went, the massacre of a sorceress was unconventional, yet undeniably exhilarating.

They turned to the object of their destruction.

"Is she safe to touch?" Ron asked, and the closest shaman nodded without stopping his chant. He patted Anong on her ruined cheek. "Guess this rich American businessman ain't as dumb as you thought, huh?" He leaned in close enough for only her to hear. "What a waste," he whispered. "I wanted to fuck you. But not now. And you know why?" He smiled. "Because you're a fucking *mess.*"

"No," she said, her voice quiet and ethereal. He wasn't sure if it was in his head or not. "It's because you love your daughter."

"What?"

"You love her... *very much...*"

Ron's mind clouded over. His thoughts evaporated, the world around him fading away, and fading fast. He... he...

"Daddy, wake up!"

What was that? It sounded like Vivienne...

Strong arms wrapped around his waist. Ron fought, but—

Jesus, what was he doing? What was he fucking doing?

His lips were pressed to those of the sorceress in a passionate kiss. Nick had a hold of him, dragging him away, as two security guards rushed to assist. Ron stumbled over his own feet and crashed to the floor.

"Are you alright, dad?" asked Nick.

Ron wasn't sure. He felt light-headed. His future son-in-law helped him to his feet, as Vivienne took up the mantle of executioner.

"Leave my daddy alone!" she screamed at the woman, stabbing her repeatedly with the switchblade. She plunged it into Anong's chest, mauling her, chunks of flesh dangling by veins and gossamer-fine tendons.

Ron grabbed her arm and stopped her. "Stand back, pumpkin," he said, and turned to Anong. "Daddy's got a job to finish." He lifted Hooper's machete and raised it high.

"You really, really love her," whispered Anong.

"Stay out of my head, you fucking witch," he growled, and spat the taste of her kiss from his mouth. He looked at her neck, and gripped the handle of the weapon.

This time, it only took one blow to slice clean through the bone.

32

Silence.

The drumming had ceased. The chanting, too, died away, leaving a group of men and one woman gathered around a dismembered, hideously charred corpse.

No one knew quite where to look.

She lay in pieces, her naked torso pumping golden fluid from where her arms and head used to be, the FUCK YOU Vivienne had carved still legible on the crispy meat.

The machete dropped from Ron's hand, and the clatter it made on the floor caused half the room to jump. He looked over to his daughter in her blood-drenched wedding dress, and only now, after the ritualistic killing was over, did he realize they should have used a replica dress for the sham ceremony.

Vivienne stared at the remains. "Don't ever fuck with my wedding," she said, and spat on the corpse. She turned to her father. "We did it. We fucked that witch up."

"Yeah," said Ron. "We sure did."

Anong's severed head glared at him through lidless eyes

as Marty Hooper approached and clapped a hand on Ron's shoulder.

"I'll dispose of her," said Marty.

"You do that," said Ron. He tasted the sorceress's vile kiss in his mouth. "Burn her to ash, then burn the *ashes* to ash. Leave nothing. I want every last trace of this... *woman* gone." He couldn't stop gazing into her eyes. Through the blood and the veins and the ragged, torn flesh, they looked somehow alive. He gestured to the shamans. "And get these guys on a plane back to Thailand. I want them out of the country and out of my life. I've wired the money to Edgar, and he'll pay them what they're due."

Anong's head glared at him. Abandoning Marty, Ron went and kneeled by it, thinking about her last words.

You love her.

He had kissed her against his will, and it took three men to drag him away.

You really, really love her.

What had she meant? Of course he loved his daughter. She was everything to him. His only living blood relative, and the heir to the Jarvis Media empire; the world was hers for the taking. So what if he wanted to fuck her in her tight little asshole? That was his divine right as—

Wait, what? What the fuck?

He winced, and looked one final time at Anong's mad, staring eyes. He stood, and booted her severed head across the room. It skidded over the wet floor and smacked hard into the wall, leaving a grim red stain.

"Mop up the blood and burn that too," he said to Marty. "Once you've done that, have the chapel sealed off."

"Sealed off?"

"Flood it with cement. Brick it up. Whatever it takes." He

wiped blood from his face. "I don't want anyone setting foot in this unholy fucking place ever again."

33

Ron showered for over an hour, scrubbing himself raw until every last trace of blood had been meticulously erased from the creases in his skin, from each eyelash, and from under his fingernails.

He bundled his clothes into a bag ready for the incinerator, then joined Nick by the window for a dram of whiskey, where they stood, appreciating the view — and the brilliant sunset that flared the sky orange — in silence.

"All this over me," said Nick, ruining the moment. "Crazy, huh?"

"Yup," said Ron. "Crazy."

"Like, this chick doesn't even know me, and she wants to kill Viv to get at me." He laughed. "As if!"

Ron finished his drink. "Well, it's over now, that's for sure."

"I'll say. You really butchered her."

"Someone had to save my daughter," snapped Ron. "I didn't see you getting involved."

"Blood makes me queasy. Whenever I see it, these

images come into my mind of me... of me doing terrible things to some woman. I don't know where they come from, or what they mean, but they mess me up, man."

"Yeah, I can't imagine," said Ron, who, unlike Nick, knew precisely what the man had done to his ex-girlfriend. If not for Ron's team, who had found him jerking off into the flames of her burning body, Nick Pulaski would be serving life behind bars right now.

Nick smiled. "It's great talking to you, dad."

"Fuck off."

He left the grinning buffoon and walked to the table to refill his glass. God, he hated him. What did Vivienne see in his empty head?

"Hey, my favorite men."

Speak of the devil.

As Ron poured his drink, he watched his daughter walk barefoot through the room, freshly showered and wearing nothing but a pink towel, her wet skin sparkling like she was sweaty from a good, hard—

"Fuck!" he muttered, tearing his eyes away from her. His glass overflowed with whiskey, and he slammed the bottle on the counter.

"Daddy? Are you okay?"

"I'm fine."

What the fuck was *wrong* with him? Sure, Vivienne was gorgeous, but... but... she was his daughter. He couldn't... could he?

No!

He closed his eyes. Something wrapped around him, and he knew it was Vivienne by the way her breasts rubbed sensually against him.

"Are you sure you're okay?" she asked. "You look funny."

"I'm fine, just let go of me." He wriggled free of her touch and walked briskly to his chair. There, he sat and stared at his knees, trying not to look at Vivienne. But, as a woman not known for taking the hint, she flopped down on the sofa opposite him. As she did, Ron swore he caught a glimpse of her pussy.

He crossed his legs to hide the emerging bulge.

It's the adrenaline, he told himself. *It's been a crazy day. You killed a witch and cut her into little pieces.*

Yeah, that was it. He needed a good sleep, with one — no, fuck it — *two* of his favorite call-girls beside him. That would settle the overactive imagination of his penis.

"You know, I was thinking," Vivienne was saying. "We should hold the real wedding in the Burj Kalifa. I love Dubai. You ever been, Nick?"

"I went there for the premier of *Space Kickboxer*. Nice place."

"What do you say, daddy? Can we do it?"

"Sure," he said, only half-listening. "I'll, uh, make some calls."

If Vivienne opened her legs another half-inch, he would see her wet, pink cunt. He thought about getting to his feet and ripping the towel from her body, leaving her trembling naked before him, covering her shapely tits with her hands and—

"You sure you're not ill?" asked Vivienne. She looked concerned. "You're sweating like a rapist."

"I'm fine!" he roared. "I just want to go to bed, is that too much to ask?" He wanted to stand, to usher them out, but his hard-on throbbed in his pants, and if Vivienne didn't get the fuck away from him *right fucking now,* he was going to come.

"Hey, dad," said Nick. "There's no need to—"

"Get out! Get out of here! Go to your own fucking suite!"

"Well," huffed Vivienne. "I guess I know when I'm not wanted."

He wasn't sure she did, but she seemed to be getting the picture.

"Come on, Nick," she said. "We're leaving."

And then, as promised, they did.

Ron remained seated until his erection subsided. Needing air, he left his chair and walked onto the balcony, letting the wind batter his face. There, he leaned over the rail, gazing down upon the streets below. This wasn't right. It wasn't normal. He felt like a teenage boy getting his first glimpse of ass, not a man in his sixties who relied exclusively on Viagra to get it up.

Jump.

The call of the void was strong. The street was far, far below him. He would probably die from shock before he hit the ground.

"Fuck *that,*" he said, and shuffled back inside, closing and locking the balcony door behind him. That witch had done something to him, he was sure of it. He took a drink and called Marty Hooper.

"Is she gone?" he asked.

"One second, let me check," the man replied. Ron heard the roar of fire, and the crackle of blistering flesh. *"Not yet. The bones and heart are the last to go."*

"Fine. Keep at it, and don't let her out of your sight. Call me once there's nothing left. You hear me? *Nothing.*"

"Will do, boss. You have my word."

Ron hung up.

Time.

It was a matter of time.

Once she was gone, whatever sick spell she had cast would leave him, and he would return to normal. He went to bed and lay shivering under the covers like a sickly child.

All he could do now... was wait.

34

Two weeks later, the wedding went ahead as planned.

It was a lavish affair, and though the Burj Kalifa was unavailable on such short notice, the ceremony took place on the palatial grounds of a Saudi Arabian resort hotel belonging to one of Ron's oil-rich friends.

The elite were there, and not even Glen Powell canceling due to food poisoning was enough to put a dampener on Vivienne's spirits. Her gown was identical to the one the witch had ruined, handcrafted in ten days by a veritable army of sweatshop workers toiling day and night for her benefit. As a generous thank you for their hard work, Vivienne had insisted on sending the workers a video message of her wearing the gown and performing dainty spins and poses.

It had been well-received, she imagined.

Throughout the ceremony, she laughed and smiled and soaked up the admiration, while the press snapped photos and filmed her as she held court over all. The sun beamed down, playing beautifully off her crystals, and for the first dance, she and Nick waltzed resplendently before the onlookers, who *oohed* and *aahed* in wonder and delight.

The day was magical, but it wasn't quite perfect.

Her father had walked her down the aisle and given her away, but after that, she had barely seen him. In fact, she was convinced he was avoiding her. Ever since that day in the chapel, he had been acting funny. He was either going senile or hiding something from her.

If it was the latter, then he needn't have bothered, for she knew all about the plane crash. The security guards were as bad as the maids when it came to gossip, and she had overheard them discussing how the private jet carrying the four black magic priests back to Thailand had been struck by lightning and crashed into the sea, killing everyone onboard. Was that the secret her father was trying to keep from her? Or was he — and this was a much more pleasant idea — planning a big surprise to end the wedding? Perhaps Ed Sheeran was going to perform live? Wouldn't that be something!

Her father sat with them during the meal, but his roving eyes never rested on her. She wondered if he was keeping an eye out for Sydney Sweeney? If so, then the joke was on him, because, like Glen Powell, she had *also* canceled because of food poisoning.

A surprising amount of guests had come down with food poisoning, it seemed.

After the meal, she saw her father one more time during the DJ set, lurking in the shadows and watching her and Nick dance with his hands in his pockets. She dragged him onto the dance floor, but he stayed for no more than a minute, before complaining of a stomach-ache and retreating to his room.

But Vivienne wasn't about to let her daddy's gastrointestinal issues ruin her special day, so she grabbed Nick, kissed him for the benefit of the cameras, and proceeded to dance the night away until her own insides started playing up.

Goddammit, she thought, as she crouched before the toilet in her and Nick's beachside villa. It seemed the food poisoning was catching, and as she vomited into the bowl, she decided to sue the catering company. First Glen Powell, then her daddy, and now her, on her motherfucking wedding day!

She stood, her head spinning, and wiped her lips, careful not to ruin her makeup. There was a knock at the bathroom door.

"Honey?" Nick called. *"You feel unwell?"*

"No, I'm okay. Too much coke, probably."

"You should do some more. That might help."

It was an absurd suggestion, but under the circumstances, Vivienne thought it worth a try. She joined Nick in the bedroom, where they cut their lines and snorted two each. It didn't help. Her belly grumbled, and she felt heavy, like she was carrying a bowling ball in there.

She lay down on the bed and turned onto her side. Nick dutifully massaged her feet, but she couldn't seem to get comfortable. She brought her knees to her stomach, and a stitch popped on her dress. Then another. An itch needled inside her.

"Unzip me," she said. Her dress, made with precision to her exact measurements, felt as restrictive as a straitjacket.

"You okay, babe?"

Why did he have to ask so many dumb questions?

"Just unzip me!" she cried, running her hands over her bulbous, distended belly.

It was funny... she swore she could feel something moving around in there.

Nick Pulaski was living his best life.

The big day was here — for real, this time — and Vivienne was finally his. Or, more accurately, *he* was *hers.* Everyone knew Vivienne wore the pants in the relationship, but he didn't mind, because sometimes he got to take those pants off, and that was all that mattered.

We'll be together forever, he had said during his vows, speaking every word with conviction. He loved her so much it hurt. Like, genuinely *physically* hurt. He ached when they were apart, and when they were together, he ached even harder.

So when Vivienne, lying on their marital bed, whispered, "Unzip me," Nick needed no further invitation.

Perching on the edge of the bed, he pulled the zipper on Vivienne's dress down with tender slowness, drinking in the leisurely exposure of her tanned skin. Despite the cocaine that raged through his body, his cock stiffened the way it always did if he looked at Vivienne for more than a few seconds.

"Would you hurry up?" she said angrily. "It hurts."

It was true. Love *did* hurt, like the old song said. He hoped this would be the prelude to some deep fucking. If she wanted to, he would be happy to fuck her all night. It meant he wouldn't have to sleep, and face the hideous nightmares that had tormented him over the last few weeks, horrifying fantasies of a burned woman offering him a dead baby, and of the lady his fiancée — no, his wife! — had hacked to pieces. The two women came to him every night in his dreams, haunting him, maddening him, until he had taken to drugs to avoid sleep altogether. At first, he used prescription medication, but quickly pivoted to cocaine when he found out Vivienne had a dealer who kept her well-stocked.

"Nick, take my fucking dress off, now!"

Maybe she really *was* in pain? Nick had assumed she was indulging in some kinky role-play, but when he heard the seams tear, and the dress begin to unzip itself from the stress, he suddenly wasn't so sure. Forgetting about the ghostly apparitions that plagued his sleep, he tore the dress from Vivienne, stripping her down to her stockings and thong. Unable to help himself, he guided his hand down the generous curves of her buttocks.

"Nick, stop it!"

She rolled onto her back, tears streaming down her cheeks, and that was when he saw it.

Her stomach... it *moved*.

The skin bulged, stretching into a balloon-like mass in the middle of her belly.

"Oh god," said Vivienne. "What is that?"

Nick, I'm pregnant.

The voice in his head spoke, and the words rang with distant familiarity. He left the bed and stumbled backwards across the room until he bumped into a chest of drawers.

"Nick, help me," groaned Vivienne. The lump slid down towards her pelvis. "Call someone! *Now, Nick, now!*"

But he couldn't. The sight of her brought memories flooding back, memories that had been locked away by god-knows-who. He remembered Carol, and the way he had pulverized her and dragged her useless flesh out to the bonfire. This was it. This was her revenge from beyond the grave, just like in his first movie, *Kickboxers From Beyond the Grave.*

"No... leave me alone!" he sobbed. "It wasn't my fault!"

"What are you fucking talking about? Help—"

Vivienne screamed. Her stomach expanded to ghoulish proportions, as something... *inside...* tried to force its way out. Five points scratched through her skin like the finger-tips of an adult hand. Another five joined them, raking across the border of her belly.

Vivienne gurgled, spluttering blood down her chin, and looked at Nick with wide, deranged eyes.

"Nick, call someone! It hurts so bad!"

Ron had been seated at the bar, far from the reception and his daughter, when he took Nick's frantic phonecall. The man had sounded out of his mind, blabbering inanities and sobbing. It could be the cocaine talking, but he also knew it could be something worse.

Much worse.

He abandoned his drink and raced through the resort as fast as his drunken legs could carry him, shoving through crowds of well-wishers and celebrity guests.

Shit shit shit.

It couldn't be happening. The shaman's daughter was dead. He had killed her himself!

"No," he mumbled, as he barreled into a group of well-dressed individuals who were openly snorting lines off the glass tables. One of them accosted Ron, who pushed him out of the way, and only as the man splashed into the swimming pool in his Ralph Lauren tuxedo did Ron recognize him as the Vice-President.

He didn't care. Right now, his daughter needed help, help that his useless, ingrate son-in-law was ill-equipped to supply. He fought his way across the dance floor, his mad dash accompanied by thumping techno beats from the speakers as licentious bodies gyrated around him.

It can't be, it can't be, he kept thinking. *We killed them. We killed them both.*

He slipped on a plastic cup and went sprawling. Two young women helped him to his feet, and he brushed off their concerns and continued onwards to the bridal suite. He should never have left them alone on their wedding night. But he had been convinced everything would be okay, and, sadly, he was unable to trust himself around Vivienne anymore.

You love her, the sorceress had said. *You really, really love her.*

Past the hotel workers he ran, as they tidied up tables and chairs and placed them in neat little stacks, and then past another pool, where several men and women frolicked nude, taking turns diving in.

"I'm coming, pumpkin," he said, his heart hammering heavily. "I'm coming!"

The blood flowed, soaking the white Egyptian cotton bed sheets.

Nick could only watch, frozen in terror, as the monstrous fingers pierced his wife's flesh, bursting through her stomach in rivers of crimson blood.

The phone dropped from his hand. Had he even called Ron? He couldn't recall. All he could hear were Vivienne's choked screams, her neck bulging obscenely as the thing inside her tried to claw its way out.

Her mouth opened wide, vomit spilling out the sides, and two bulbous, wriggling worms reached out over her jaw.

No, not worms.

They were fingers. Human fingers.

More joined them, gripping Vivienne's teeth and dislodging them, the roots tearing her gums open and flooding her mouth with blood. Her cheeks bulged so far that the skin became translucent, her pores widening from tiny pinprick holes to bloody rents in the flesh. The fingers pushed further, wrapping around her jawbone and pulling, until an entire hand protruded from between her lips.

Nick fell to his knees, weeping and begging, as one-by-one, Vivienne's ribs cracked, the bony shards bursting from her chest and tearing her breasts apart, loose flaps of bloody tissue dangling from the ends of the splintered ribs. And inside, between frayed cords of skin and vein, and nestled amongst muscle and putrid entrails, grinned a face he had never seen before; that of an old man with a wild, victorious expression, covered in blood and a white sticky substance.

Nick, I'm pregnant.

"It wasn't my fault," he sobbed.

But it was when the second face emerged from between Vivienne's legs, ripping her vagina apart, that Nick truly, irreversibly lost his mind. For this woman he *did* recognize.

Vivienne, her legs and fingers twitching, split up to her navel as the woman pushed herself free from her fleshy prison, the skin tearing like it was being unzipped. She slid out of the torn carcass and landed on the floor with a thump, her nude body slick with blood. She stretched like a cat, and turned to Nick. He averted his eyes, his gaze falling on his wife's face. Two wizened hands protruded from her mouth, her cheeks splitting into a hideous rictus. Her skull cracked, blood and mangled brain flooding from her nostrils, and then the old man inside her savagely tore Vivienne's head in two.

Nick stared blankly at the carnage. He knew he should feel repulsed by the grisly spectacle, yet he had committed worse atrocities in his time.

"But it wasn't my fault," he said, and pointed at the naked, newly born adult woman on the floor. "She *made* me do it."

∾

Ron was close.

The waves of the Red Sea crashed against the shore, and he found his progress impeded by the soft sand underfoot. He stomped across the beach, his feet sinking with each tortured step. The building loomed ahead of him, lit only by the ambivalent glow of the moon and some fairy lights strung around the balcony rails. He kicked off his stiff shoes and continued on. Woozy from the exercise and the alcohol, he jogged up the steps that led to the front door. He couldn't stop now. Not when his pumpkin was in danger.

Inside, the villa was silent.

"Vivienne?" he called as he entered the hallway. "Nick? Where are you?"

"Good evening, Mr. Jarvis," came the reply. *"We're so glad you could make it."*

"Oh god," groaned Ron, the fight leaving his body. He staggered into the villa and fumbled for the switch. The downstairs exploded in yellow light, revealing Suwin and Anong together on the bridal suite loveseat. The pair were covered — literally drenched from head to fuckin' toe — in blood, and as a final, cruel insult, they wore the happy couple's wedding clothes. Nick's tailored suit was comically oversized on Suwin, loose around the neck and chest, with baggy sleeves that hid his hands, while Anong wore the tattered remains of Vivienne's gown, the blood turning it a lurid shade of scarlet.

Ron trembled, holding the wall for balance. He looked at the shaman with disbelieving eyes. "We killed you."

"True," said Suwin. "And yet, like a bat out of hell, here I am." He smiled. "You really should have killed both of us."

Ron turned to Anong. "But we *did*. I killed you myself, in the chapel."

Anong chuckled. "You honestly thought I'd fall for that trick from *Bikini Voodoo Kickboxers?* Mr. Jarvis, you must give me more credit than that."

"It's a good movie," said Suwin. "But I didn't think much of the sequel."

"Jesus," Ron groaned. They were insane. Everyone was insane. "What have you done to her? What have you done to my baby girl?"

Suwin smiled. "Don't you like surprises, Mr. Jarvis? Go to her, please. See for yourself."

Defeated, Ron shambled past them, a sharp pain stabbing into his heart.

"Wait," said Anong. She rose from the seat. "My father may be done with you, but I'm not."

Ron stopped, his head bowed, tears filling his eyes. "What now, you fucking monsters?"

"Earlier," said Anong, as she stood before him in Vivienne's dress in a sick parody of his daughter's special day. "At the fake wedding. We never finished what we started."

She grabbed him by his lapels and pulled him close,

kissing him. Ron didn't fight back. He was too tired, too confused, too scared. Anong broke the kiss, then tore a strip of blood-soaked fabric from the wedding dress. She waved it in front of his eyes, then forced the rag into his mouth.

"Swallow," she commanded, and he obeyed.

They had beaten him. For once in his life, Ron Jarvis had lost.

Anong whispered indecipherable words into his ear, then stroked a hand down his cheek.

"It appears our deal is complete," said Suwin. "Now go to your daughter. Show her you love her. Show her you care."

Anong smiled. "And you do love her, don't you? *You really, really love her.*"

Ron stumbled backwards. "You stay away from me, you hear?" The taste of his daughter's blood contaminated his mouth. "You stay away from my family!"

"And you, Mr. Jarvis," said Suwin, "would have been wise to stay away from *mine*. But it's like you Americans say, isn't it? All's fair in love and business."

With the man's mocking laughter in his head, Ron turned away and followed the bloody trail the pair had left. It led through the hallway to a flight of wooden stairs, then up the steps to a long corridor and, lastly, to a closed door.

Ron placed his hand on the wood and prepared himself.

"Vivienne? Are you in there?"

He pushed the door open.

"Good god," he uttered.

35

THE POLICE CAME EARLY THE NEXT MORNING, ALERTED BY A maid who had discovered the blood while delivering a basket of fresh fruit to the bridal suite. Resort Manager Tony King, Ron's close personal friend and business associate, was in bed when they arrived, still a little drunk and still a little high.

Marge, a sweet young woman he had hired as his secretary because of her cute tooshie, had banged on the door for five straight minutes until he answered. When she told him what was going on, Tony hadn't bothered to get dressed. He stepped into his slippers and raced from his room in his robe and underpants to intercept the cops. He needed to stall them to give his staff enough time to sneak into the bridal suite and *hide all the fucking blow*. Tony's resort was well known among the elite as the kinda place where nothing was off-limits, even in the notoriously strict Saudi Arabia. With his private airstrip, he could import all the drugs and hookers he wanted, shipping them door-to-door from his Florida compound.

And now the fucking cops were coming.

"Don't let them in!" he shouted at his secretary. "And hide the hookers!"

"Where do you want me to put them, sir?"

"I don't know! Take 'em for a goddam sightseeing tour for all I care, just get 'em outta here before we're shut down for good!"

He ran through the lobby, dodging suitcases and ignoring the irate cries of one of his regulars, a US senator with a penchant for cocaine and golden showers, though not at the same time.

He spotted Fred Rubert, his head-of-staff, standing in the driveway.

"Fred! Where are they?"

The man's face was pale. "I tried to stop 'em, Tony. I tried to stall 'em."

"Where are they? Where are the fucking cops?"

Fred shook his head and jerked a thumb towards the beach.

"Shit," said Tony. "Ready the jet. We might have to make a quick getaway. Make sure Marge is onboard."

"Which one's she?"

"The one with—"

"The cute tooshie, right." Fred nodded. "I'm on it."

Tony left the man to make the arrangements and raced after the cops. The authorities had been sniffing around for months, looking for an excuse to close the resort down, and only steady — and steadily *increasing* — payments to the local police force had kept him in business.

But now that might all be for naught.

The cop car was parked by the beach. Tony ran to the cruiser and peered through the window. The vehicle was unoccupied. He looked towards the bridal villa where Ron's daughter and her husband were staying, and wondered what the hell was the matter. Had Vivienne snapped and killed someone? He wouldn't put it past her. The chick was a firecracker, no doubt about it.

With the sun on his back, Tony headed across the beach, following the footprints left by the cops. He saw them on the porch, talking to a woman in a navy resort uniform. Probably the maid who had called them, he figured.

That moron.

"Hey!" he shouted. They didn't hear him. He waved his arms. "I'm the manager, and everything is under control!"

This wasn't going to end well. He considered running back, boarding his jet, and flying straight home to Florida. But he had sunk a lot of money into this place, and he wasn't about to let it slip through his fingers just because Ron Jarvis couldn't keep his daughter in check. And anyway, if the incident was purely drug-related, he could probably bribe the cops to keep their mouths shut.

The officers headed inside.

Cursing all the narcotics that coursed through his body, Tony reached the villa and leaned on the porch rail, catching his breath. He glared at the maid, muttered, "Clear out your locker," and hauled himself up the stairs and into the suite.

The first thing he noticed was all the blood. It pooled on the floor, and stained the sofa and carpet. Something big had gone down. He heard footsteps, and ran through the hallway, avoiding the bloody puddles and catching the two officers as they reached the top of the stairs.

"Guys, wait up!"

The officers paused, allowing Tony to catch up to them. They looked at him expectantly, and he noticed one of them reach for his gun.

"Woah, woah, fellas! I think there's been a misunderstanding."

"Who are you, sir?" the first officer asked, his fingers grazing his firearm.

"Name's Tony King. I own this resort, and I apologize that you've been called out on a false alarm."

"A false alarm? The woman downstairs—"

"Is old and confused," said Tony, forcing a knowing smile.

Unimpressed, the officer glanced down at the bloody carpet, then met Tony's gaze. "So what's that?"

Tony had to think fast. "What? Oh, the *blood*. Don't worry about that, it's all part of the theme. The newlyweds in that room," he said, pointing to the closed bedroom door and lowering his voice, "are very important people, and they love a good horror movie. They make them, in fact. You ever see *Lesbian Kickboxers in Transylvania*? No, guess they probably didn't show that one over here. Never mind. What I'm saying is, the blood is just food coloring, that's all. To make the wedding feel like a horror movie."

"Food coloring?"

"Yeah," said Tony, beads of sweat forming on his forehead. "Food coloring."

The cop stared intently at him. "Prove it."

Tony chuckled, then realized the man was serious. "What do you mean, prove it?"

"Taste it. If what you say is true, it's only food coloring."

"But it's... it's on the *floor*."

The cop crossed his arms, while his partner turned towards the bedroom door.

"Fine!" said Tony. He crouched and ran one finger through the red smear, then held it up for them to see. Were they really gonna make him go through with this? He put his finger in his mouth and sucked it clean. Unsurprisingly, it tasted like blood.

"Mmmmm." he said, curling his toes. "Delicious."

One of the cops laughed. He patted Tony on the shoulder. "Okay. I believe you."

"You do? I mean, uh, great! Again, boys, I'm sorry to have wasted your time. Say, why don't you fellas stop by reception on your way out, and I'm sure we can furnish you with some expenses for—"

The bedroom door opened, and all three men turned at once.

"Ah, *shit,*" said Tony.

A disheveled, nude young man stood hunched in the doorway, blood dripping down his face and legs and heavily muscled torso. Tony recognized him as Nick Pulaski, movie star and husband of Vivienne Jarvis. They had snorted coke together in the men's room last night.

"It wasn't my fault," said Nick.

"He's an actor," said Tony, thinking on his feet. "He's playing a role."

The cops weren't listening. They manhandled Nick to the ground, and despite his size and supposed martial arts skills, he refused to resist, lying on his stomach while they snapped cuffs on him.

Run, Tony. Get out of here.

He would. But Tony was the kind of guy who slowed down at traffic accidents to see the bodies, and who used to import snuff pornography from a dealer in Scotland. He was, as he would happily admit, a fucking sicko, and he just *had* to see what Nick Pulaski had done to his new wife. So, while the cops dealt with the unhinged movie star, Tony sidled past them into the honeymoon suite for a cheeky glimpse of the bloodshed.

When he entered, the leering grin dropped from his face.

"Oh boy," he said when he saw his old friend Ron Jarvis. The man was naked, and at first Tony thought he was humping the bed, and that the blood was Ron's own. But then he realized that the flattened, soggy sheets were actually a person, and that Ron was fucking the shattered corpse of his own daughter.

Vivienne.

She had been ripped open, her stomach and chest shredded, her intestines spilling out of the grotesque cavity. Her face was a mangled, bisected horror, the jaw dislocated and hanging to one side. Ron squeezed a breast in his bloody hands, but it wasn't attached to anything.

It had been torn off.

Vivienne's cracked ribs pierced his own skin, locking the two bodies together as Ron gripped his daughter's cold, dead thigh, sliding his hand to the torn hole between her legs and fingering the sagging flesh, wetting his fingers in her blood.

"It's not my fault!" Nick shouted from the hallway.

"Ron," Tony said. "You... you gotta stop that."

His old friend turned to him, his mouth twitching into a smile. He picked up a handful of Vivienne's guts and sniffed them. "I can't," he said, and licked the intestines, running his tongue over their foul softness. He was crying as he spoke. "They put a spell on me."

Tony threw up. It was the smell more than anything. Of dead flesh, and of feces, and of blood and vomit and entrails and cum.

"They put a spell on me, I swear!"

Tony looked from the puddle of his vomit to the grisly vision of his old friend penetrating Vivienne's remains.

"Ron," he said, wiping his mouth. *"Please."*

The cops entered. They grabbed Ron and hauled him off his daughter. His cock was red with blood, and as hard as a rock. He fought back, shaking free and throwing himself atop his daughter in a harrowing spectacle of incestuous desire.

"Vivienne," he cried. "Oh, Vivienne! You're so beautiful!"

The officers wrestled him onto the floor, and as one radioed for backup, and the other cuffed his wrists behind his back, Ron turned to Tony with tears in his eyes.

"I love her," he said, and uttered a bloodcurdling shriek. "Don't you see? Don't you understand? *I really, really love her!"*

AFTERWORD

Thank you for reading Death Spell, and I hope you enjoyed it, you sicko.

This book came about when I kept seeing people refer to my books as 'extreme horror' or 'splatterpunk.' With a couple of exceptions, I've never really thought of my books as particularly extreme or gory — maybe Satan's Burnouts or God's Hand, up to a point — so I was curious to see what I would come up with if I actually tried to write something utterly disgusting with no redeeming social value.

As usual, my initial plan took a few unexpected turns on the way to completion. What started as a nonstop wallow in gore and depravity soon took on a more satirical aspect, especially once I got a handle on the cast of grotesque assholes populating the story. 'John Waters meets Herchell Gordon Lewis' was how I pitched it to myself, a high-camp gorefest that only occasionally removes its tongue from its cheek.

I originally planned to release this book on the same day as Summer of the Monsters, as both are about father/daughter relationships and yet sit at opposite ends of the horror spectrum. Where Summer is sweet and tender and quiet, Death Spell is brash and cruel and outrageous. It would have been a fun double bill, but also a pretty terrible marketing decision.

~

Thank you Heather, just for being you.

Belly rubs for Boris, who is settling into life as a senior pug by acting like a big puppy all day, every day.

Huge shoutout to Maciej Kamuda for his epic cover art.

Cheers to Steve, Connor, and Elli for their assistance and support.

Commiserations to my mother, who I know will read this book even though I asked her not to.

And thanks to you, dear reader. Have I told you lately that I think you're super-mega-ultra cool?

SUGGESTED WATCHLIST

If you enjoyed this book and wish to further explore the
wild world of black magic films, here are some of the ones
I've enjoyed the most, with my favorites in bold. Please be
aware, some of these regrettably contain scenes of real-life
animal violence, so proceed with extreme caution.

Magic Curse (1975, Taiwan)
Black Magic (1975, Hong Kong)
The Oily Maniac (1976, Hong Kong)
Black Magic 2 (1976, Hong Kong)
Mystics in Bali (1981, Indonesia)
The Queen of Black Magic (1981, Indonesia)
Bewitched (1981, Hong Kong)
Sundel Bulong (1981, Indonesia)
Centipede Horror (1982, Hong Kong)
Red Spell Spells Red (1983, Hong Kong)
Devil Fetus (1983, Hong Kong)
The Boxer's Omen (1983, Hong Kong)

Seeding of a Ghost (1983, Hong Kong)
The Hungry Snake Woman (1986, Indonesia)
The Seventh Curse (1986, Hong Kong)
Roh *aka* Spirit (1989, Indonesia)
The Eternal Evil of Asia (1995, Hong Kong)

EXTRA SPECIAL THANKS TO MY PATREONS

Adam Soll
Anna the Cheddar Goblin
Audie Schultz
Brendan & Honey Bunny
Brendan Fitz
Brittany Ross
Courtney Pearson
Danielle Chiarappa Perkowitz
Destinie
Elli Wade
Eric Rumsey
Hannah Orr
Isaiah Woodyard
Jarrod Linehan
Jason Zuriff
Joctan Hernandez
Josh Heaps
Joshua Carter
Kala Vining
Luke Martin

Matt McCleland
Mel Kaye
Meredith Jensen
Michelle S
Miss Kitty Fantastico
Nicola Swordy
Nicole Stephens
Noah Andruss
Peter Jilmstad
Phoebe Thompson
Rebecca Vale
Robert L
Rochelle Hennings
Ryan Orgel
Sarah Brown
Sebastian Ersson
Steve Stred
Tyler Geis
Vickie Allan

ABOUT THE AUTHOR

David Sodergren lives in Scotland with his wife Heather and his best friend, Boris the Pug.

Growing up, he was the kind of kid who collected rubber skeletons and lived for horror movies. Not much has changed since then.

His best known books include the gory and romantic fairy tale The Haar, the blood-drenched folk-horror Maggie's Grave, and the analog-horror fever dream Rotten Tommy. David also writes under the pseudonym Carl John Lee, publishing splatterpunk novels such as Psychic Teenage Bloodbath and Cannibal Vengeance.

instagram.com/paperbacksandpugs

ALSO BY DAVID SODERGREN

The Forgotten Island

Night Shoot

Dead Girl Blues

Maggie's Grave

The Navajo Nightmare (with Steve Stred)

The Perfect Victim

Satan's Burnouts Must Die!

The Haar

And By God's Hand You Shall Die

Rotten Tommy

Summer of the Monsters

Writing as Carl John Lee

The Blood Beast Mutations

Horror House of Perversion

Cannibal Vengeance

Horror House of Perversion 2: The Slaughtered Lambs

Psychic Teenage Bloodbath

Death Freaks on Hell's Highway

Psychic Teenage Bloodbath II

CONTENT WARNINGS
(MAJOR SPOILERS)

Violence and gore (torture, murder, mutilation,
dismemberment)
Rape, assault, and sexual violence
Animal violence (chickens, toads, worms)
Domestic abuse
Castration
Necrophilia
Immolation
Suicide
Infanticide
Incest

Made in the USA
Coppell, TX
20 June 2025

50655638R00152